CHRISTINE HART

The Electric Girl

First edition

ISBN: 978-1-7775194-0-7

This book was professionally typeset on Reedsy.
Find out more at reedsy.com

To John and Betty for always making me laugh.

Acknowledgement

Although this story was written a few years ago, revising and editing during the 2020 pandemic presented unique stresses. Publishing now would not have been possible without the help of a few key people.

Warmest thanks to Andrew Wilmot for their thoughtful assistance in honing my world-building and filling in my supporting characters.

Thank you to fellow moms Shavawn, Dianna, and Tatiana for being my sounding board during this book.

And thank you to my husband Jeff for his overall supportive nature, in my creative work and as a life partner.

Chapter 1

Childish things have a way of resurfacing when your heart is torn in half. Polly Michaels hadn't played with her Lite-Brite for years, but now the little glowing dots brought her comfort. She wiped a tear from her cheek and carefully poked another clear peg through the black construction paper on top of the plastic screen. Warm yellow-white light instantly filled the peg. She dabbed her dripping nose and sat back to examine her work: two luminous blue and white clouds floating over a shining rainbow, and a unicorn mid-gallop. She felt a small twinge of contentment. The little circles of light gave clumsy definition to the unicorn's features, but Polly could picture the animal fully in her mind.

She glanced at the collage of hand-drawn unicorns on the wall behind her desk—charcoal profiles and pencil crayon landscapes depicting the mythical creature over and over. Large and small, detailed and rough, Polly had been drawing them for years. Every time she decided to take the drawings down, trying to convince herself to grow up, she found she couldn't bring herself to let go. She had never been able to do justice to the image in her head. Now, however, it felt better than ever to keep her mind's eye focused on something so beautiful and pure.

Polly held the image of a perfect glowing unicorn in her mind and then looked back at her bubbly light peg version. Her chest tightened and she

"

punched the side of the Lite-Brite with all her might. The plastic box went flying, knocking her cup of loose pegs onto the floor, a colorful spray of tiny pieces. Satisfaction mingled with regret in her gut and acute stinging on the knuckles of her right hand.

Oh no, the noise! What if I woke her? she thought.

POP! . . . POP-POP-POP!

Something much louder outside her window snapped the night's silence like dry twigs.

What was that? Gunshots? In the orchard? It couldn't be.

Polly looked out her window and saw, off in the distance, a crackling dome of electricity blooming over the long rows of cherry trees beside her mom's renovated farm house. The energy burst with a *BANG*, releasing a thick beam of frosty light into the sky. The light pivoted erratically as if searching the sky for something. With a swift sweeping motion, the beam bathed Polly in blinding white light. She slammed her eyes shut and dropped to the ground, curled into a ball.

The light went out again. Polly waited, listening for . . . something. She opened her eyes. Swirls of color danced on a black background—she blinked, struggling to clear her sight. She sat up and pressed her face against the window, waiting for the trees to catch fire or for the electric dome to return. She refused to blink again. Not until the spectacle made sense.

Another *POP-POP-POP* and the bright dome reappeared a beat before light once more shot up into the sky. Dryness pulled at Polly's lips; she couldn't stop gaping. Instinct froze her every muscle.

This is dangerous. Go check on her.

"Mom!" Polly ran down the hall to the other end of the house.

She's asleep. She's okay. I'm okay. It's just a helicopter . . . or something.

She threw open the door to the master bedroom. Sure enough, her mom was still sound asleep in bed, exhausted from the day's chemotherapy session. Her soft auburn hair looked steel-gray in the moonlight. The black-and-white checker-board comforter glowed like an exotic cocoon around the rest of her mom's body. The velvet tiger in the painting above the headboard stood frozen in a tense crouch as though guarding her.

Polly walked over to her mom's dresser and pushed the red button on top of the ghetto blaster. A loud click stopped the cassette, ending a gentle rush of ocean beach noises. The dresser was covered in dust, hair ties, receipts, and costume jewelry. Polly caught sight of the mood stone earrings she gave her mom last Christmas. The flimsy pewter setting on one had bent by accident in her mom's hand, so there they sat, waiting for a repair that would never happen. Polly rewound the ocean tape to the beginning. If her mom woke up needing to barf, Polly wanted to make sure the soothing sounds were ready to go again when she came back to bed.

Polly retreated to the hallway to regroup. She walked past the main bathroom and the spare bedroom-turned-art studio. At the top of the stairs, Polly froze. She badly wanted to investigate the orchard, but her mom's fear of coyotes and bears roaming the hills ricocheted between her ears like a warning.

Mom will definitely freak out if she catches me outside at night. But it's not like she'll be getting out of bed—not to come looking for me.

Polly crept softly downstairs and into the vaulted kitchen. In the window behind the double sink, her mom's stained-glass butterfly reflected a glint of moonlight. Her gaze darted from the window to the sliding glass doors across the room, behind a small round oak table. A greasy takeout box and two plates of chicken bones on the counter—her mom's only half-eaten—glistened in the faint light. She paused next to the table, gripped the padded back of a dining chair, and leaned toward the glass door. She peered out, across the backyard and into the orchard.

A large beacon of light flickered in the trees. It moved, as if floating. No, not floating—walking. The intense glow, marked by dark strips of trunk and branch, moved at a measured pace. She squinted, trying to make out an outline of . . . whatever it was that meandered through the trees.

It's an animal. It has to be!

She lifted the latch on the sliding glass door and gently opened it. Chilly night air rushed in, smelling of ozone and the earth. Her flannel nightgown billowed in the breeze. She placed a bare foot on the smooth concrete of the patio. The cold was sharp and shot straight through Polly, causing her to gasp, but she forced herself to keep moving. She stepped all the way out and slid the door back into place, almost closing it but not quite.

The roving light in the orchard had grown larger. It was weaving between the dark rows of trees in the distance. The undulating pace of it . . . it wasn't human. Whatever it was, it was moving—walking, she thought, but not on two legs.

Polly put one foot in front of the other, compelled by her need to know. She crossed the backyard, reaching the bumpy bare earth of the orchard floor. She steadied herself against a tree trunk as adrenaline raced through her veins. She leaned into the tree, hoping to conceal her figure without losing sight of the creature, whatever it was.

She waited, watching in both awe and terror as the glowing animal came closer. The creature made no sound at all. Polly watched, eyes trained on the glow itself, until finally she could make out a shape—a long, muscular torso flexed above four knobby legs. Pointed ears flickered.

It's a horse! A white mare! Oh my god, she's so bright.

The horse turned its head, flashing a spiraled horn—unmistakable against the dark branches around them.

NO WAY!

"Polly? Are you out there?" she heard her mom call. She turned to see her mom's silhouette standing in the kitchen. Her mom flicked on a light, spilling yellow across the yard. Polly whipped around to see the unicorn again, but the orchard had grown dark, full of silent indigo trees.

The glowing animal was gone.

Chapter 2

Steamy air turned the sandstorm swirling around Sy'kai into a gritty paste that stuck to her scaly skin. She looked down to shield her lidless eyes and clenched her large jagged teeth as she slid along the surface of an unfamiliar world. Wing-like appendages flapped against her elongated body as she moved. Pain pulsed through her strange muscles as the injuries from another failed battle slowly healed—bruises fading, wounds stitching themselves together. She squinted into the grainy brown mess, desperately searching for some form of shelter that would allow her the respite needed to open a new fissure in the fabric of spacetime.

Clusters of giant quartz shards punctuated the landscape of cracked dry mud and clumps of brittle yellow grass. The orange glow of the planet's enormous sun blasted through breaks in the sandy clouds, intermittently turning the crystal outcroppings into flashing lamps. Sy'kai narrowly missed colliding with shard after shard as she fled, nearly blinded each time.

Why not end it here, sssssssister? said a voice in her head. A flicker of recognition set her mind ablaze, the words "brother" and "extinction" bubbling to the surface in a reptilian language that her brain was still learning. Sy'kai knew the strange speaker immediately: Nur-gahl, her nemesis. They were the only two morphlings left in existence. If she could finally defeat him, she would be the last. The safety of the Astral Temple and its ocean of precious knowledge would be assured. "Hsss, hsss, hsss"—the sound of alien laughter cut through the thumping air and sent a chill through Sy'kai's bones. If *he* defeated *her* instead . . . She shut her eyes—it was an unthinkable outcome.

She stopped to catch her breath. Immediately, she sensed a gigantic form behind her. It enveloped her suddenly. Hot pain cut into her neck and thick green blood flowed down her ridged chest. She fought to free her body from Nur-gahl's fierce jaws and talon-tipped arms.

Nur-gahl released her from his shallow bite and repositioned himself, ready to lunge, to land a killing blow. Sy'kai's body, slick with blood, slipped from his hands. She found her leathery wings again. She slithered away furiously, flapping and concentrating until she could get her wings moving in unison, and she took to the air. But she managed to remain airborne for only a few seconds before plummeting back down.

"I will not die here!" Sy'kai shouted into the storm. She turned her head as the wind shifted, driving a blast of sand into her lizard face. Her throat throbbed; blood grew sticky on her wings.

"You are wrong! Again!" Nur-gahl belted. His voice was close, inside her head. *I will kill you and feed on everything on this planet. And once I have your energy and abilities, I'll move on to a new world. And then another. I will feed on all life that I find until the universe is a void.*

Panic pulsed through Sy'kai's veins. They had only been on the alien planet for two days—her transformation into a domestic life form was barely complete and already she was near death. Nur-gahl seemed to find her more quickly in each new world. Her memory was still patchy while his wits were as sharp as ever. Having chased her through the portal instead of tearing one of his own—something he was physically incapable of doing—Nur-gahl suffered none of the neurological side-effects that plagued Sy'kai. She mulled over the futility of her situation and his never-ending advantage over her. Her body tensed and she balled her tacky finger-like claws into something like fists at the tips of her two front wings.

"We will see about that!" yelled Sy'kai as she caught sight of a jagged boulder creating a small lee in the storm. Sensing Nur-gahl mere paces behind her, Sy'kai pushed herself forward until she made it to the small sanctuary provided by the rock, and then collapsed. She took a deep breath and focused all her mental energy through her front wings, out through her claws.

Sparks cut the space in front of her, dancing in a lacy ice and sapphire ring. *If I can close the portal with him inside, it won't matter what we leave behind or where I land.* Trapping Nur-gahl was nearly impossible because Sy'kai needed her wits about her to close a portal. If she closed it too quickly, Nur-gahl would be left behind, free to devour an entire world, unchallenged by beings not capable of understanding what he was let alone the depths of his hunger, his fury. With every new passage her brain grew increasingly muddled by the energy expenditure and the instant intake of information—the new world and all its life being taken in at once. Her only chance to weaken and then destroy Nur-gahl was to find a world at the moment of its death, with nothing left for him to mimic. Sy'kai focused every molecule of her consciousness on finding this elusive destination. Her electricity stretched into a clumsy oval as a window to the unknown tore open. Energy exploded outward. Fresh, sweet air rushed at her, filling her lungs with relief.

But this new world was far from barren.

"I smell a feast on the other side! Go ahead, jump in. I am right behind you, ssssister!"

Rage flared in Sy'kai's core. She risked a glance back and saw the dark silhouette of a gargantuan, monstrous creature racing toward her. She faced the portal again and plunged through.

Heat and light devoured Sy'kai's flesh as the fissure enveloped her. *What will I be on the other side? Please, please, let this be the final shift,* she thought as the vacuum of the portal crushed her entire being.

Nothingness.

And then she was spat out from the portal, into the dark of night. Atoms pulled other atoms into minute clusters as millions of electric implosions sucked matter off the ground and out of the surrounding terrain. Pure instinct flowing from a primal mind scanned the landscape for a blueprint of sentient life. A mental tentacle scraped and slurped, hungry for material until it finally latched onto something in the distance and made its decision. Another explosion crackled behind her elemental brain, but the sound hardly registered in the morphling's still-forming body.

Gray matter coalesced, bone materialized, and muscles knit themselves around the skeleton as it built itself from nothing. White light and raw energy found purchase through four glowing hooves. Delicious soft gas kissed her forehead, a body part that felt somehow heavy. Light hovered overhead, illuminating the way forward through dark leaves and moist dirt.

Brightness flooded the field ahead of her. Moments later, as her eyes adjusted, she sensed another life form somewhere inside the light. Instinctively, she walked toward a face she couldn't see. A slight figure, a willowy bipedal creature with orange-red hair slowly came into focus. And the morphling brain, still crude with instinct and ability, reached out telepathically to evaluate this opposing alien heartbeat.

She turned back to the trees then as she felt the heat of another uncontrollable transformation taking hold.

Chapter 3

"You're missing the Gummi Bears, Polly!" Her mom yelled from the master bedroom on Saturday morning. A cheesy song about bouncing bears echoed down the hall.

"Seriously, Mom, why are we watching cartoons?" Polly shouted up the stairs.

"Because you love them and you know it!"

Polly walked slowly, concentrating on balancing two plates loaded with eggs, hash browns, and fresh fruit. She thought briefly about telling her mom what she'd really been doing outside last night. A good night's sleep had dulled the shock, but Polly still felt a nagging need to understand what she'd seen.

"Hey, if kid shows make you feel better . . ." Polly said as she entered the bedroom. She grinned as she handed a plate of food to her mom. Polly's stomach sank as the inevitable voice in her head chimed in: *You better soak up all this fun now, while you still can.*

They ate as they watched the colorful medieval-themed cartoon. Polly ate faster than her mom, who had to set her unfinished food aside after a few bites. Her mom lay back and propped herself up on her pillows to continue watching.

"Get over here and snuggle your sick old mom." She spoke as though she had a cold, nothing more, and was simply feeling needy. Polly fought back tears as she stared at the fuzzy thirteen-inch television balanced on the dresser, avoiding her mom's sunken eyes. She nuzzled into her mom's shoulder, trying to think of anything but losing the only family she knew.

"I'm feeling better today. And Doctor Johnson told me my white blood cells are bouncing back like champions. He's pretty confident I'm going to beat this thing."

Polly watched the cartoon bears bicker playfully. "Mom, Stage 4 lymphoma isn't something you beat like the flu. Even I understood how serious this was when we first got your diagnosis."

"Then you remember Henry telling us that my chances were good."

"I heard fifty percent for five years."

"That would only get me halfway through your college years. No good. I'll have to hang on at least seven years to make it to your graduation." Her mom chuckled her way into a cough.

"That's not funny." Polly sat up and crossed her arms. *Will I even be able to finish college if Mom dies halfway through? Will I want to . . . do anything?*

"I don't think it's funny, dear, but we have to be able to talk about this. It's my job to make sure you're prepared for everything life throws at you." Her mom's voice grew quiet. "Including my death."

"I wish you'd been one of those super-religious types." Polly sighed.

"Why? You think this would be easier if we could blame God?"

"If I could just picture you waiting for me in Heaven, I might even be happy for you. Caroline Chu's family is like that."

"Did her mother tell you I would be happier there?"

"She did use the phrase 'going to a better place' when I told her. And then she gave me that plate of peanut butter cookies to give to you." Polly felt a now-familiar—and hated—lump forming in her throat.

"Well, never mind Caroline's mother. I'll take *her* a plate of cookies when I'm through this treatment." She extended her arm and Polly snuggled back in. Polly rolled her eyes, humoring her mom. "Are the girls still coming for a sleepover tonight?" her mom asked, clearing her throat.

Polly flinched—she was nervous about whether her mom could handle a house full of teenagers right now. "Yeah, I'm pretty sure they're still coming."

"Good. You need something fun to take your mind off everything. I won't have this disease erode what's left of your childhood."

Polly batted away the retorts that came to her. Nothing she could say would actually do any good. Both she and her mom had wrestled with their inability to "fix" this whole cancer situation. They had been a team for so long, and her mom had always approached their problems with a can-do, pull-up-your-socks type of determination. Cancer wasn't playing ball, though. They had to do everything the doctors advised and simply hope for the best while wringing their hands.

Two months had passed since a mystery flu and a blood test turned into a biopsy—which landed Polly and her mom in a doctor's office for the worst conversation of their lives. Their town, Bella Vista, was so small that they knew Dr. Johnson personally. The Johnson twins, Bethany and Brittany, would be at Polly's sleepover. So, dealing with her mom's cancer behind closed doors would never have worked out, although only Polly had wanted to bury the truth like that. She hadn't wanted her mom to get a biopsy in the first place. At the time it felt like having that test was an invitation for illness to slip in the back door and devastate them by surprise. Polly thought the words *I told you so* over and over in her head, despite not having actually warned her mom off getting the biopsy. The idea had also occurred to her that if her mom wasn't going to get better, what good was all this miserable chemo? The kinder thing—for both of them—would be to let the disease run its course peacefully: one day her mom simply wouldn't wake up and Polly would mourn, but they would be spared this long, drawn-out parade of misery.

"What are you thinking about, sweetie?"

"That we're unlucky." Polly looked up and into her mom's face while the television switched to an ad for cake mix.

"How do you figure? Other than my having cancer."

Polly looked out the window and into the clear blue sky above the trees across the street. Everyone else in Bella Vista was enjoying a perfectly simple Saturday. Every single one of her friends and classmates had either two parents or a nice big extended family. No one else had a dying mom. Polly thought again about telling her mom she'd seen a unicorn. There was no way to say the words, though, without her mom questioning Polly's sanity.

"We lost Dad in a stupid car accident. You had to drop out of college when you got pregnant. We don't have enough money to fix the awning over the sliding door in the kitchen. I can't stop thinking about how much of your savings you're burning through with chemotherapy. When—if—you get better, are we broke after that? It seems like there's always going to be something wrong. No matter what we do."

"I know it seems like everything is broken right now. But this is just a bump in the road. I promise, you won't always feel the way you do right now. Life is always going to challenge you, Polly. It's how you respond that counts."

"I've got a response for cancer—this!" Polly flipped her middle finger at the ceiling.

"There you go! That's what I think of it, too." Mom laughed.

Polly stood up and gathered up their plates. "I'm going to the store to get party supplies. Do you want anything?"

"Just your warm little smile."

Polly obliged her mom and kissed her on the forehead before leaving.

The sun poked through the clouds as Polly's bike coasted around the corner onto Lakeview Road. She enjoyed the ride into town, crossing the rural land around her orchard-adjacent home. Getting home wasn't as much fun—pedaling uphill until she could taste blood—but the future seemed further away when fresh air flowed over her, the valley before her stretched wide.

Bella Vista's largest supermarket was a Safeway at the end of Main Street. Polly could have stopped at a corner store closer to home, but she wanted to indulge in the sorts of large bags of junk food she could only find on big chain shelves. She parked her bike in the rack outside the Safeway and patted her backpack to make sure she'd remembered her wallet.

"Hey, Polly," said a tall boy in a black leather jacket as he strolled through the automatic doors and into the supermarket.

"Hey, Nick," Polly said, managing a strangled reply. Her throat was parched following the bike ride. By the time she'd finished slurping from her water bottle, Nick Hauser was long gone. She stowed the plastic container back in the metal sleeve on her bike frame. Nervous heat danced in her chest, crawling up to her cheeks as she pictured running into Nick's chiseled, handsome face again inside the store. She took a deep breath and entered, grabbing a wire basket by the door. *Snacks and pizzas. Just get snacks and pizzas*, she said to herself as she marched, head down, to the frozen food section.

"Hi, Polly!" a cheerful girl's voice startled her. Alya Sanon was suddenly standing beside her, smiling with dark, excited eyes. "Are you getting stuff for the slumber party? I am. A couple of bags of chips or something. I'm totally excited! My parents hardly ever let me do sleepovers. But now that *my* mom is starting to talk like *your* mom is—" Alya stopped mid-thought, mouth open. She didn't need to finish her sentence. The whole town knew about Polly's mom. If they weren't sending them proverbial cookies, they were, of course, sympathetic, supportive, praying, and so on.

"It's okay—don't worry about it. Mom is doing really great. We had a nice big breakfast this morning. Everything's fine." Polly knew she didn't sound convincing, but it felt good to say the words anyway. She looked up and down the aisle for Nick, seeing only a few elderly ladies examining the shelves.

"That is so great to hear, Polly, so great." Alya's huge natural ringlets sprang up and down as she bounced with relief.

"Mention the Mom update to Caroline and the twins, please, if you see them. I don't want everyone showing up tonight tiptoeing through the front door. It makes things harder." Polly clenched and released her jaw.

"I will. And we won't, I promise. See you later!" Alya waved and jogged off to finish her own shopping.

Polly glanced to the end of the aisle just in time to see Nick's dashing smile flash a group of small kids as he exited holding a paper bag in his arms. In a perfect world, she'd find him waiting for her in the parking lot, leaning up against the side of his massive red pickup. He'd wave her over, open the door to let her in, and throw her rusty old bike in the truck bed.

Polly stood in line with her basket and gazed out the window at Nick's truck as he tore out of the parking lot without looking back and drove in the opposite direction. He had forgotten about her completely.

Chapter 4

The pale girl woke, the sour odor of decaying fruit and dew-soaked earth wafting over her face. The scents were completely alien to her, as was the sensation of air lifting the hairs off her damp skin. She sat up.

What am I now? Where is this place?

Slick leaves slid off her arms and back. Black shapes danced menacingly across a ceiling of dark blue above. Thick organic pillars crinkled and shifted as though whispering secrets. The girl had a vague sense that huge swaths of important knowledge were missing from her brain. She put her hands to her face, evaluating her features with her fingertips. Then she paused to examine the hands themselves.

This must be a fascinating world if this is the dominant life form.

The girl's legs wobbled as she stood. She held out her arms for balance, allowing her mind and muscles to get better acquainted. A long, thick ribbon of pale blonde hair flowed down her back, swaying with her every movement. Twigs and leaves were snarled into the fine strands. She shook her hair, failing to knock the debris loose, and a piece of information hit her:

I am called Sy'kai. There it is! I knew I had a name. That is a start. This language is going to take some getting used to, I can tell.

Heat and ripples of pain radiated up from Sy'kai's arm. She lifted it to look—sticky dirt coated a deep red slash under her bicep.

How long have I been here? Did I receive this injury from the landing? Did I shift twice? This mental fuzziness is worse than usual.

Sy'kai looked at her naked, ghostly white body. Her lithe limbs shivered in the cold. She draped her massive amount of hair forwards and back again until she achieved some semblance of warmth.

I need to orient myself before I start investigating. Where are the other life forms in this realm? Do I want to be near them or as isolated as possible? My retrieval gland—of course!

Sy'kai jerked her head as she remembered the biological device implanted somewhere under her skin. She searched her new body frantically, desperate to see the device's faint pink glow. Her right palm rewarded her. She flexed her hand and held it up for closer inspection, spotting the soft light just beneath the surface. Satisfied, she pinched the middle of her right hand with the thumb and forefinger of her left and pressed as hard as she could and, finally, a blinding flash and a wave of nausea knocked her to her knees.

Blue-green bile poured from her mouth as images and sounds flashed through her mind one after another, over and over again. She saw massive structures of stone and colorful accents alongside simple wood buildings. Expansive fields of cultivated plants gave way to unruly tangled forests stretching from sea to sea. Metal machines crawled like creatures; swirls of paint told stories of grand empires and poignant love and vicious conquests. All building upward from one generation to the next, over and over. This world housed a wealth of variety, and an advanced species capable of art and engineering. The visual and auditory onslaught continued long after the contents of Sy'kai's newly formed stomach were gone. Her mind's eye went dark—the voices stopped chattering. Sy'kai became aware of her body convulsing, slowing to small shakes and spasms. Her breathing became regular again and the throbbing between her temples relented enough for her to sit back up.

Holy crap, this Earth place is complex! And young! Radical, dude! Wait, what does that mean? Oh, why did I not wait for my original knowledge bank to stabilize before completing formation? I will not remember properly for days now!

Sy'kai punched the ground hard, angry at herself and the physical pain she'd endured, only to further confuse her situation. A flicker of recognition grabbed her attention as her gaze came to rest on an empty ice cream pail at the foot of a nearby tree. She looked up at the branches above, full of small, glossy orbs. Another piece of information slipped into place like a tingling gear in her head.

Cherries! These are fruit. I am surrounded by food! And that container or "bucket" is for collecting food. Good, that will help me recover.

A rumble of hunger erupted from the girl's gut and she ran to the plastic pail. She picked it up and looked inside. A handful of leaves were stuck to the inside. Another gear turned.

Hmmmmm. That is plant matter. Edible, but not nutritious.

Sy'kai examined the leaves in more detail and knocked out the pail's contents. Using her fingers, she frantically wiped the plastic interior as clean as she could before grabbing handfuls of cherries from the low-hanging branches. The bucket was soon full, and Sy'kai sat with her back to a tree trunk to eat.

Ow! Vicious seed!

Sy'kai spit out a cherry pit and assessed her traumatized molars with her tongue. Nothing felt damaged, but frustration welled in her chest and she felt water filling her eyes. She sobbed and ate cherries until she fell asleep.

CA-RACK! A resounding break woke Sy'kai with a jolt. Panic launched her to her feet. She was still groggy, feeling surges of disorientation from her center of gravity up through her throat. She scanned her surroundings for signs of life in the dark orchard.

How long was I asleep? That noise, it must have been close to be so loud. What was it? A branch snapped off one of these trees? By what?

Sy'kai took a deep breath and searched the terrain around her with her mind, employing greater control this time. Images of creatures floated through her: antlers, fangs, fur, and claws all surfaced along with foliage and terrain for the semi-arid desert region. She picked up impressions from each animal's image; some were predators, but most were grass-grazers and insect-eaters. The plant life outside the cultivated fruit trees was a mix of dry sagebrush and old pine trees. Her remote vision sailed over grassy hills, coming to a rocky cliff above a turquoise-emerald lake.

I need to find somewhere safe and secure to wait out the absorption of this realm along with my memory's full return. It will not do to climb one of these trees. I need a structure. Something fortified to some degree.

KABOOM!

Whatever is making that sound, I hope it cannot smell this body.

Snarling and snapping erupted in the distance, along with heavy thumping footfalls that shook the ground. Sy'kai felt her new heart beating out of control. She strained to pinpoint the source of the threat. It had to be coming from the west. She bolted east, running hard until she tasted iron in her mouth.

A light appeared in the trees ahead. She stopped, slipping behind a tree to hide. The predatory sounds had vanished, but Sy'kai was still too afraid to move. She heard burbling noises. Voices.

What are those things? Or who? Is that how the language that's now in my head is spoken? Can I trust them? I must not risk myself!

She caught sight of a pile of wood propped against the tree next to her and slipped over to it for a better hiding place. Throbbing pressure pumped through her body. Sy'kai fought to calm herself as she flattened her naked body against the tree and prayed for every living thing in the woods to back far, far away. She took a deep breath, then another. She narrowed her eyes as she composed herself.

I am stronger than this. Nothing will take my life today. I am ready to fight.

Chapter 5

Polly adjusted her arrangement of jellybean, M&M, and mini marshmallow dishes into a perfect triangle at the center of their circle. Overflowing bowls of chips and cheese puffs, along with the eager faces of her friends, waited patiently. The basement was quiet, except for the hum of the furnace in the back corner. Each of the girls had their flashlights ready, on, and pointed upward.

"I hereby call the tenth meeting of the Blondie Girls to order." Polly nervously retied the copper-red ponytail on the side of her head. Forcing her friends into a club was starting to feel as silly as owning a Lite-Brite and saving unicorn drawings. But she had something more important than coolness to talk about tonight. She shifted the neckline of her favorite sweatshirt, the one with the awesome picture of a pink, orange, and yellow Miami sunset.

"Does anyone else think that name is starting to sound dorky? We're in the tenth grade now." Alya leaned in to slurp from her grape slushie. She pushed her tortoiseshell glasses back into position.

"I don't really listen to Blondie anymore," said Caroline.

"Sacrilege!" said Bethany.

"Actually, I'm more into Pat Benatar now," Brittany said while staring at the worn shag carpet.

"Should we even play music tonight? I mean, if your mom is trying to rest and all." Caroline's voice was soft and sympathetic.

Polly looked at Alya and then at each face in the circle around her. Alya's father worked at a local lumber mill while her mother stayed at home. Caroline's parents owned a restaurant that they lived above. Bethany and Brittany's parents worked together at Bella Vista's small hospital—their father was the chief physician and their mother was an ER nurse. In spite of what each girl believed about their worldliness and maturity, Polly was certain that none of her friends had ever been touched by personal loss.

Polly had recently developed a bad habit of chasing bitter moments with waves of resentment. Not only did her friends all have healthy moms, they all still had dads, too—nice men who loved them and looked after them. If her mom died, Polly would have zero family in her life.

Polly's dad had left his family on the other side of the country—they were not good people, from what he'd said. If the worst happened and she hadn't reached legal adulthood, unless the government—or whoever—could find her mom's sister, Aunt Flora, Polly would become a ward of the state. The term made her sound like a criminal—like it was her fault her mom was dying. She pushed all of that turmoil further down, into the bottom of her belly, with a single deep breath.

"I don't want to talk about music or Mom. I saw something in the orchard last night. And we're going to check it out. Now."

"Hold on. Was it an animal?" Alya arched her eyebrows.

"Kind of," Polly said slowly.

"What do you mean 'kind of'?" said Caroline.

"It wasn't just an animal. There was something . . . It was like an incident. I think." Polly watched the expressions of confusion and concern form around her.

"This *does* sound interesting." Brittany scooped a handful of jellybeans without taking her eyes off Polly.

"Can we have a little more detail before we go wandering off into an orchard at night, next to wild hills full of whatever?" Alya said as she leaned into the circle.

"I don't think it's a good idea at all," Caroline said, frowning. "Especially since you're so isolated out here. Your nearest neighbor is a fifteen-minute walk by paved roads. Nobody's around if we need help." The hint of fear in her voice grated on Polly's nerves.

"My mom says the hills are probably full of coyotes," said Bethany.

"My dad actually hunts not far from town. He brings home a deer at least once a year, and he says he's seen fresh animal kills out there," said Alya.

"There are no aggressive coyotes around here," Polly snapped. "I mean, we hear them, but they never come into the yard. I've never seen any dead animals. And I'm not sure if it was an explosion or some kind of industrial accident. But there was a huge bubble of electricity. And a white horse. With a horn. It was beyond bizarre." She focused on the glittery stars in the galaxy poster on the wall in front of her to avoid making eye contact with anyone.

"What? Are you serious? You're saying you saw a unicorn? A UNICORN!? Have you lost your marbles?" Brittany tilted her freckled face to the side, trying to catch Polly's eye.

"It's obviously a prank," said Bethany through a smirk.

"Why would someone pull a prank like that? And who'd do it?" Caroline scratched her head, genuinely intrigued.

"Never mind the fake horse—you said there was an explosion. Did you call the cops? What did they say?" Alya sat back but held her stare.

"Of course I didn't call the cops. That's the last thing I need around Mom right now." Polly glared at Alya. "I don't know anything else. The only way we'll figure it out is to go look ourselves. So who's coming?"

"I'm not plodding around that orchard at night," said Caroline firmly. She pushed her long straight hair back and sat up straight.

"You do realize we could get shot at for trespassing." Alya's dark eyes widened. "If you're set on going, I'd better come with you. I've got the best set of ears in the room—I'll hear whatever's out there before it gets to us."

"We'll go!" Brittany nodded at her sister and stuffed a few more marshmallows in her mouth.

"Speak for yourself, nutcase!" Bethany flicked a jellybean at Brittany.

"I'm not making anyone do anything. Alya, Brittany, you come with me.

Caroline, Bethany, you guys chill out here until we get back. I'm pretty sure Mom's down for the night." Polly stood up confidently.

Bethany and Caroline looked at each other. Neither wanted to encounter Polly's mom, should she end up wandering the house in a drugged and confused state. But Polly didn't give them time to contemplate. She grabbed her denim drawstring backpack and marched up the stairs with Alya and Brittany on her heels.

Bethany slipped her sweatshirt over her head and stood up. "I'll come, too. Someone's got to be ready to run back here and call the cops."

"As if I'm going to stay here by myself." Caroline rolled her eyes and launched herself forward to catch up.

The girls found their shoes as Polly slid the glass door at the edge of the kitchen all the way open this time. She marched across the small patch of grass that separated her property from the edge of the orchard. The lawn ended and lumpy earth took over, covered by damp orchard debris. Rotting leaves and wet twigs scrunched under Polly's sneakers with each step forward.

The evening air wasn't as chilly as the night before. A slim band of vivid azure clung to the horizon behind the wiry trees, black stalks under the twilight sky. A tinkling sound came from behind. Polly whipped around to see Alya tying up her hair. She glared.

"Sorry. I'll take them off." Alya slipped the gold bangles off her wrist and stuffed them in her pocket. "It's good to let animals know you're coming though."

"How far do you want to go, Polly?" Caroline leaned around Polly, trying to get a better look at the land in the distance.

"Shhhh!" Polly frowned.

"There's nothing out here. My feet are freezing." Brittany hopped back and forth in her pink jelly shoes.

"You shouldn't have worn beach shoes to a slumber party in the hills," Bethany whispered angrily at her sister.

"Wait, there is something out there!" Alya blurted. She jabbed a finger straight ahead. Polly stared into the dark, desperately trying to find where

Alya was pointing. Suddenly, a flash of white dashed between two trees.

"That's not a horse," said Bethany as the girls picked up speed.

"No, but it's pretty weird!" Brittany pushed past the group and ran ahead.

"Brittany!" Polly cried out. She chased after her friend.

Brittany ran until she'd arrived at the spot where they'd seen the moving white shape only moments earlier.

"There's nothing here," said Caroline. Her voice trembled as her eyes darted in every direction.

Polly and the others scanned the orchard, taking in all angles. Moments passed. The only sound they heard was the rustle of wind through the trees and the heavy breathing of the five of them.

Polly took a few steps toward the nearest tree and laid her hand on the cool bark. She saw a ladder and a stack of weathered wood crates propped against a tree in the row ahead. She walked over to it. The hair on her arms and neck stood at attention—prickling energy surged in her chest, spreading out to her arms. Each step gave a loud *SMUNCH*, despite her trying to tread lightly. She reached the ladder, gripped the edge, and pulled herself around to peek at the other side.

A slim albino girl, naked and terrified, looked back at her. Her eyes, like a frozen winter sky, grew rounder and wider. She stepped back from the tree, shrouded by a cloak of white hair, and opened her powder-pink mouth and let out a blood curdling EEEEEEEEEEEE!

Polly threw her hands up over her ears to block out the sound. Her eyes slammed shut, but she forced them open again and glanced at her friends, all of whom had their hands on their heads, pain evident on their faces.

Polly whirled back around in time to see the albino girl sprint away, into the trees, a blur of platinum hair and bare skin.

Chapter 6

Sy'kai ran deep into the orchard, angling herself away from the figures that had come from the light outside the trees. Finally, she found a structure with a door, somewhere she could hide properly, gain time to think—and, hopefully, to remember.

This will have to suffice. I only hope the wall panels do not obstruct the sound of something approaching. You can trust this space, Sy'kai, you are concealed and safe, she thought, coaching herself into the sense of calm she needed to evaluate her surroundings.

She waited for her new eyes to adjust to the faint light inside the rough little building. Sy'kai touched the wall and let her fingertips learn from the wood. The word "shed" jumped into her brain. A piece of fabric resting on a shelf came into focus. She picked it up and unfolded the thick material as the words "tarp" and "canvas" joined her growing vocabulary. The fabric was stiff but large enough to cover herself with, so she wrapped it around her body like a tube and tied a dirty rope around her waist. The makeshift dress was not comfortable, but her torso was now covered and the fabric's rigidity kept it from folding down.

She reached for a small clear box and examined the spools she found inside. A sharp splinter of metal stuck out of one—recognition jarred again in her brain.

This is for creating garments. But I can use it on my arm. That should speed healing, too. Good. Was that water I saw outside? I can only hope.

Sy'kai stepped back out of the shed and plunged her injured arm into a barrel of rainwater next to it. It was nowhere near sterile, but instinct urged her to clean her wound before closing it.

Back inside the shed, an overturned crate tucked in the corner provided a place for Sy'kai to sit. She threaded the needle and took a deep breath before piercing her skin at the top of the gash in her bicep. She breathed sharply with each draw of the thread, but she had the wound closed in only a few minutes. The pain eased back down to a nagging throb and Sy'kai rubbed her face.

Slow down, you need peace for this.

She focused on feeling the movement of the fluids in her muscles. She listened to the air moving in and out of her new lungs. Once she felt centered, she pressed the retrieval gland in her hand again.

Swirls of color flashed behind her closed eyes: stories, events, numbers, art, faces—all flowed into and through her mind. Rivers of chatter in dozens of languages competed with the sounds of animal cries and the squeal of machinery. A wave of nausea rolled over Sy'kai. She breathed deeply to keep it from crashing into her body and ejecting the small amount of food she had consumed. Satisfied, she released the subdermal device and listened to the wind outside the orchard shack. She closed her eyes again and reached out with her thoughts, searching for the red-haired girl. A pale, lightly freckled face filled the blackness of Sy'kai's vision. She relaxed her concentration once more and it faded.

The first shift . . . that image, the white horse with a horn. That came straight from a nearby mind. How unusual! The young female human who saw me, she has those pictures in her room. She truly loves that animal . . . but it does not actually exist on this plane . . . the shift could not hold. This body . . . the second shift did not successfully complete. I will stand out among these people until I can summon the energy to adjust my pigmentation.

Sy'kai activated her gland once more and began to flip through the images it produced with precision that improved by the moment. Without warning, a black blur composed of malevolent power engulfed her, sapping her vitality and stealing her breath. Sy'kai opened her eyes as the terrifying memory of the creature hunting her came into focus.

Nur-gahl. He followed me through the portal. What form did he take here? How deadly is he now? Where is he? Sy'kai took another deep breath and let out a long sigh. *As long as I am incomplete, Nur-gahl may decide to hold his attack, waiting for restoration of my full power before he tries to take it from me. I may still have time.*

The snapping of twigs sounded in the distance—Sy'kai focused again on where she was. She leaned against the shed wall and placed her ear on a seam between two uneven wood planks. A soft breeze rustled through the thousands of leaves outside. Suddenly the crunching and snapping started again, accompanied by heavy thumps and guttural growls. The noises grew in volume as they rolled forward. Whatever it was, it grew louder . . . closer. She had to make a break for it.

Sy'kai sprang through the shed door, sprinting toward the homes that lay outside the orchard. Her pursuer followed, quickly gaining ground, monstrous feet pounding the earth behind her like a boulder crushing its way through a forest.

The cherry trees gave way to an overgrown field so thick that Sy'kai had to peel off her tarp to move quickly. Naked again, she reached the edge of the tall grass and met a wood plank fence surrounding a huge yard. She looked one way and then the other. She was smack in the middle of the barrier—both routes around would take too long. Not wasting another second, she gripped the top of the wood plank in front of her and yanked hard, pulling with every ounce of adrenaline-fueled strength she could muster. The nails in the wood released their hold and the piece came off. Sy'kai squeezed through and scanned the yard ahead of her.

A few fruit trees and a small gazebo on an overgrown lawn stood between her and the back of a quaint stucco-and-brick rancher on the other side of the yard. She could see no useful place to hide. Despite the growing brightness of the sky overhead, the home's windows were still dark and there was no movement inside that she could see. A steel drum on the other side of the yard caught Sy'kai's eye.

She sprinted across the lawn, a streak of white flesh, and lifted the lid of the drum to peer inside. The vessel could indeed hold her entire body. Inside she saw her reflection in a calm pool—more rainwater. She tried to push the drum over, to dump out the icy water, but it wouldn't budge.

The thundering mass of snarling rage behind her had found the gap in the fence. A huge hairy muzzle of sharp teeth snapped through the opening she'd left. She had no choice—Sy'kai heaved herself up and into the drum, reaching for the lid at its side before plunging into the frigid water. She pulled the lid shut and folded her limbs inward, praying that she had concealed her scent—and that her body could withstand the cold.

"What, exactly, do you suggest we do now?" demanded Alya as Polly carefully shut the sliding glass door from the safety of her kitchen.

"Shhhhh! You're going to wake up Mrs. Michaels," Caroline snapped. Polly didn't have the heart to correct her use of "Mrs." for the umpteenth time.

"Maybe it *is* time to call the police." Polly eyed the phone on the wall reluctantly. If she made the call, they'd want to talk to an adult.

"How about the hospital?" Brittany said. "Dad isn't working tonight, but Mom is. She might be able to send a paramedic."

"To do what, shine a flashlight into the trees?" Bethany scowled at her sister.

"Polly is right. It has to be the police." Caroline looked to Polly, offering support.

"Do you want me to do it?" Alya offered. Polly could sense the empathy in her voice.

"No, it's my house, my problem. I mean, it's my responsibility." Polly picked up the phone and dialed 9-1-1, tapping her foot nervously as the rotary dial clicked around again and again. It was the first time she had ever made an emergency call.

"Nine-one-one, what's your emergency?" asked the operator.

"I need to report a lost and injured girl. At least I think she's injured." Polly looked around at her friends' alert expressions, pressing the mustard-yellow receiver against her face as the operator asked for her name and location. "Polly. Polly Michaels. It was in the orchard behind my house. On Sagebrush Ridge Road. She was naked and very pale with white-blonde hair. She screamed and ran away into the trees, but I think she's still there. It's the Lakeview Hills Cherry Orchard." Polly hung up then and let her shoulders droop. The whole exchange felt rather anticlimactic. White noise danced between her ears.

"Well . . .?" said Alya.

"Are they coming?" asked Bethany.

"The dispatcher—I don't think she said her name—she's going to send a patrol car to our street and down to the orchard's storefront in the morning. They're not coming right away."

"Why not?" Caroline frowned.

"She sounded a bit . . . I don't know. Like she didn't believe me. Like she was humoring me. I thought she'd want to talk to Mom, but she just asked who I was, where, and could I tell her what the girl looked like."

A pregnant pause hung between them.

"Maybe this didn't really qualify as an emergency," said Brittany.

Polly's heart sank at the thought. She worried that her friend was right and that she had overreacted. Obviously, she hadn't really seen a unicorn—it was, in reality, a homeless and potentially mentally ill albino girl. Maybe it was the strain of waiting for her mom to get better or . . . Maybe her brain had tricked her with such a vivid hallucination. Maybe she had been more spooked than she realized during the electrical storm and her eyes weren't working right.

"We should get to bed," said Caroline.

"There's not much else we can do." Bethany touched Polly's elbow gently.

Polly wanted to rip her arm away from her friend's fingertips, but she knew it would be an unjustified and ungrateful gesture. Instead, she nodded and led her friends back down to the basement to unroll their sleeping bags.

The next morning at breakfast, Polly's mom joined the girls while sporting uncharacteristic wild hair, a stained nightgown, and dry, chapped lips. Her rounded shoulders combined with the shuffle of her slippers made Polly want to order her back to bed. The girls were all wearing T-shirts, sweatpants, and flannel, with varying degrees of disheveled hair, so the contrast in wellness wasn't too dramatic. But Polly noted that the bags under her mom's eyes had deepened. She wanted her mom to finish her coffee in the living room, at least until her friends went home.

"Polly, would you be a dear and get the morning paper from the front step?"

"I'll get it Mrs. Michaels," chirped Caroline. She was up and out of the room in a beat.

"Did you girls hear the storm the other night?" Polly's mom managed a playful smile as she looked around at her daughter's guests.

"Mom, how did you manage to hear that?" Polly cut herself off before commenting on her mom's exhaustion. She straightened her flannel shirt as an excuse to look down.

"You bet we heard it!" Alya said with enough enthusiasm to dislodge her glasses. She quickly shoved them back up the bridge of her nose.

"We actually went outside last night to look for—" Brittany paused, realizing she couldn't finish her sentence without making Polly sound like an idiot. She adjusted her oversized shirt.

"The lightning strike," Polly added, glaring at Brittany. "In the orchard. I saw it outside my window, but I didn't say anything 'cause I didn't want you to be scared." The cover story rushed out of her like spilled milk.

"Well that's a sad turn of events, the daughter protecting the mother. I must be in a sorry state to have you worried like that."

"Here you go, Mrs. Michaels." Caroline happily dropped the *Bella Vista Gazette* on the table in front of Polly's mom. Her flawless black hair swung back and forth like a pendulum as she thrust the roll of paper on to the table.

"Whoa, it looks like someone managed to get a photo!" Alya leaned out of her chair to get a better look at the cover story.

"'Electrical Storm Still Shocking Town.' Boy, they don't miss any puns." Bethany eyed the photo as she took a big bite of a toaster waffle. Polly's mom smiled at Bethany and turned back to the paper.

"After consulting with experts in Vancouver and Seattle, local meteorologists say the light show was due to a pyrocumulus cloud. The bizarre phenomenon, also known as dry lightning, could signal the start of an early forest fire season for British Columbia and Washington. Following up on our original coverage of this incident, Bella Vista residents are advised to—" suddenly her mom clamped her hand over her mouth and rushed upstairs.

Polly heard the bathroom door slam shut followed by the muffled yet unmistakable sounds of retching.

"We should probably head home and let your mom get some rest," said Caroline. Polly ignored her, reading the rest of the *Gazette*'s cover story.

"I'll call my mom. She could probably take us all." Alya reached for the phone on the wall.

"No, wait!" blurted Polly. She snatched the receiver from Alya's hand. "The paper says they're sending government investigators to confirm that there isn't something weird or illegal going on." Polly looked at each girl as she clung to the paper in one hand and the phone in the other.

"Isn't that what we want them to do?" Caroline tilted her head.

"Maybe they'll find that albino girl, too," Bethany said, nodding.

"What if they do? I can't explain it, but I don't think government agents or scientists will help that girl. You guys didn't see her face. There's something weird about her. It was in her eyes. I think she's . . . different."

"She sure has a healthy set of lungs—we all know that." Alya crossed her arms.

"Couldn't we just *try* to help her?" Polly stopped short of adding, *Please, if I can't help my mom, I could help that girl instead.* She hung up the phone and stowed the paper on top of the china cabinet.

"Polly, I know you mean well, but what could we possibly do for a lost, naked, probably not-right-in-the-head runaway from who-knows-where?" said Caroline.

"My parents might be able to help. If we can find her, we could take her to our place," Brittany gestured between her and her sister.

"Mom and Dad are not going to want us bringing some escaped mental patient back to the house," Bethany said, holding up a hand to her twin sister.

"Let the cops—or whoever—pick her up and take her to the hospital. They can treat her there."

"Wouldn't it be easier to find her and ask what happened? If we can talk to her, maybe she can tell us what she needs." Polly gave each girl a pleading look. Her hazel eyes appeared wet with anguish. The sound of Polly's mom throwing up caught their collective attention again.

"I suppose we could take a walk through the orchard and see what we find," Alya said, shrugging her shoulders. "Might as well put all that Girl Guide knowledge to some practical use."

"Sure, I guess. My parents aren't expecting me home until this afternoon." Caroline's tone wavered. "I did want some time to work on my flower pressing project, but that can wait."

"Ugh. I suppose we're in, too. But let's pack a lunch and dress warm." Bethany looked sideways at Brittany, who was already grinning. "I sooooo hope we find this chick. I bet she's got one hell of a story."

Chapter 8

Sy'kai listened to the slow rhythmic beat of her heart as sensation faded from her hands and feet. Instinct forced her to flex her fists and wiggle around while hugging herself. Determination drove her to keep this fragile new form from expiring in a metal drum.

What will happen to me if I die in this body? Will I be trapped here? If only I could remember.

A vision formed on the backs of Sy'kai's closed eyes. Tiny white sparkles twinkled like glitter glued to dark paper. Pinkish-purple haze flowed in a ribbon before her, coalescing in spots, swirling into blinding white orbs. The new language taking root in her brain assigned a word to this cosmic tapestry: home.

Sy'kai opened her eyes. She felt an unsettling disconnect between herself and the nebula-like image fading quickly from her mind. How could that be home? So much information was still missing. She contemplated using her retrieval gland again to find answers or accelerate her mind's healing. As long as she needed to remain hidden, the risk of a seizure giving away her position was unacceptable. She reached out mentally, hoping to detect no thoughts around her, signaling that it was safe to climb out.

After what felt like an eternity, she decided to trust the silence and forced her rigid form to stand. She lifted the drum's lid and crawled out into the morning air. A gentle breeze sent daggers of cold across her flesh.

She looked around the yard again, this time pausing to search for usable items rather than calculating threat assessment. A clothesline hung between her and the large picket fence. Sy'kai pulled down a pair of pants and a sweater. She put on the clothes and started rubbing her limbs to get warm, but it was not enough. She had to get indoors and close to something warm. Around the side of the house, a square of clear substance close to the ground looked like a discreet point of entry. She felt slowly around the frame and the words "window" and "basement" popped into her head. Another tingle in Sy'kai's brain informed her that such an opening would be locked.

She retreated to the seating area in the backyard to find somewhere to regroup. She caught sight of a pair of large black foot coverings there, near an entrance. They were too big and her feet flapped up and down as she walked inside the cold material, but the alternative was bare sensitive skin on the hard ground. She assessed the rest of the exterior. A bench with a thin cushion rested against the wall. Sy'kai folded her body into the seat and massaged her limbs again, to try and improve what circulation she had.

Time passed painfully slowly as Sy'kai struggled to warm herself. Her stomach burbled with greedy juices, willing her to get back up and look for food. *I need something substantial. What does this space have to offer for nourishment?* She crept toward a small shed, far nicer than the one she'd stumbled into in the orchard. *Perhaps this building holds more items. Should storage next to a home not be a trove of goods?*

"Not one more step, kid," said a menacing, husky voice from behind.

Sy'kai whirled around, coming face to face with a long black stick with two metal tubes. An elderly man gripped the device by its wood base. The way he pointed it at her face suggested it was a weapon.

"I . . . am . . . I . . . need . . . help . . . please." Sy'kai struggled to speak, both from the cold rapidly shutting down her body and the awkwardness of using this new language aloud for the first time.

"You need to stand right where you are until the cops get here. I watched you wandering around out here naked before you stole my wife's clothes. She's on the phone with the police right now. I don't know what you're playing at, but we don't take kindly to thieves around here. You picked the wrong place to squat." The man's narrowed eyes were full of hate and disgust—she'd recognize those emotions in any creature.

Sy'kai lifted her arm instinctively, hoping to allay his anger.

"Don't even move," said the man.

"I . . ." Sy'kai searched for the words to defend herself. Her pulse increased. Her stomach twisted. "No."

"I swear to God, kid, if you don't shut up and stand still, I will shoot you. You're trespassing, and I'm well within my rights." The man's rage swelled as he spoke.

"Please," she said softly. As Sy'kai spoke, she sensed gas moving out through the palm of her extended hand. A faint distortion in the air puffed forward until it hit the man's face.

He sniffed and squinted as though smelling something strange. He stepped back, perplexed, swinging his gun back and forth through the gas now streaming at his head. The man coughed, gasped, and fell to the ground unconscious.

Sy'kai looked at her hand, mystified as to how she had produced a gaseous substance capable of incapacitating her captor. A siren entered her awareness then as she smelled the air around the man. Out of the corner of her eye, she saw the long entrance panel in the home open outward.

"ELMER!" shrieked an old woman who had appeared in the backyard. "What have you done?" The woman picked up the man's long weapon and pointed it at Sy'kai.

BEEEE-OOP, BEEEE-OOP—the siren wailed even louder. The crunching of gravel ripped into the ground as a car came to a stop on the other side of the wood wall.

Sy'kai looked at the frightened old woman, then to the latched gate where she knew something or someone would burst through any second.

Decision made, she lunged forward and sprinted back to the gap in the fence.

"Hold it! Don't run! I'll shoot," yelled the woman, but Sy'kai knew it was an empty threat. She felt the woman's fear and total unease at even touching the weapon.

Rapid thumps pressed against Sy'kai's lungs and ribs as she ran, back through the fence, back into the orchard where Nur-gahl was probably still hiding, waiting for her.

Chapter 9

"Is there any chance someone's parents will call here? Or worse, show up?" Polly glowered at each of her friends in turn as she stuffed cookie packets and wrapped muffins into her backpack. "Call home and check in if you need. I can't have worried parents getting Mom all worked up."

"Relax. Our parents are all giving your house a lotta space right now." Alya immediately regretted both her word choice and irritated tone. They all knew that Polly was well aware of the unending flow of pity directed at her house from half the town.

"If we're seriously doing this, we need a plan. That girl might not be lucid," said Bethany. Brittany nodded in agreement as she, too, finished packing her bag. "Yeah, my mom says disoriented people can still be wicked strong. She might try to lash out before we get a chance to talk to her. We should be ready to jump back if she thinks we're dangerous."

"We all saw her. She's terrified, not malicious. Besides, what would we do, hit her?" Caroline turned to Alya and added, "Even those of us with bloodthirsty hunters for fathers don't necessarily have that fighter's disposition." Alya glared back at her with wide, scandalized eyes.

"I'm sure she's had a chance to calm down by now. She'll be cold and hungry. That's enough to take the edge off whatever confusion she felt. We could take a baseball bat if it makes you feel better," Polly said to the twins.

"If we get weapons involved, I'm going home. On foot if I have to. Sorry, but I just can't get into some kind of fight." Caroline shifted uncomfortably from one foot to the other.

"Who said anything about weapons? Something like pepper spray would be fine. Have you got anything like that?" Brittany looked around the kitchen.

"Ummmmm . . ." Polly scanned the cupboard. She opened a drawer and lifted a long can. "We've got bear spray for when Mom goes hiking."

"Perfect." Bethany accepted the can from Polly.

"Be careful where you point that thing. You guys are lucky I'm here, you know." Alya crossed her arms. "My 'bloodthirsty' father taught me how to track animals in the forest. An orchard isn't much different. I'm not an expert, but I'm better than most fifteen-year-old girls."

"I know. We all know, and we're glad you're here." Polly shot Caroline a reprimanding look.

"Do you think we can really help her?" asked Caroline.

The faint wail of a siren caught Polly's attention. "Does anyone else hear that?"

"Yeah." Bethany was suddenly on alert, too.

Polly froze. "Maybe it's the police finally coming to look for our girl. I don't know if they'd bother with a siren for that. It could be an ambulance. There's an elderly couple down the hill. Maybe one of them fell."

"Or had a heart attack." Brittany popped a piece of muffin in her mouth and chewed.

"As long as no paramedics are coming here—I can't deal with that right now." Polly zipped her bag shut. The other girls avoided eye contact. "Did everyone get enough to eat?"

"I think we're full," said Alya.

"Plus, we all took some snacks." Caroline reached around and patted her pack.

Brittany nodded, mouth still full. Bethany rolled her eyes.

"Then let's get moving." Polly opened the sliding glass door and the group went out into the backyard and headed toward the orchard.

They quickly found the spot where the albino girl had been hiding behind the wood crates and ladder the night before. Alya began examining the scene and Brittany looked as though she was biting down on a caustic critique.

"If I remember correctly, she ran south down the hill. It doesn't look like she came back here during the night." Alya retraced her steps around the area to be sure. "Our best bet is to follow her trail south and see where it leads. If she got all the way to the edge of the orchard, she might be hiding in a yard or a tool shed just off Lakeview Road."

"Wait, do you think the siren was for the naked girl?" Caroline's eyebrows arched in consideration.

"Don't worry, once we find the end of the trail, we'll keep our distance." Polly shivered at the image that popped into her mind all of a sudden—of the strange albino girl being strapped down in the back of an ambulance.

Alya led them through the orchard with Polly right behind her. The girls picked their way across the damp ground as carefully and quietly as they could. The air was taut with shared caution, and they refrained from making small talk. Soon, the girls reached a wood fence missing a board. Alya gestured that they regroup out of view of anyone that might be in the yard.

"I don't see anyone in there, but this damage is fresh. Look at the exposed side of the wood here. It was pressed up against something else until recently." Alya pointed to bright brown strips on the inside of stained gray planks.

"Do you want me to sneak in and look around?" Brittany leaned toward the gap, doing her best to get a look inside.

"No! Absolutely NOT!" whispered Caroline.

"We do need to know." Polly peeked into the yard, keeping all but the top of her head concealed. "I don't see anyone, but we shouldn't just walk on in. We can go around and approach from Lakeview Road. I'll knock on the front door and tell them the truth. Or most of it."

"Wait, don't bother," said Alya, no longer whispering. She plucked a few strands of long platinum hair from the raw edge of the wood and then scanned the back of the house from one end to the other. "The house is dark and quiet. Nobody's home. And it's not worth it to waste time—or risk meeting an angry neighbor from one of the other houses on this road."

"Thank goodness for common sense." Caroline's shoulders drooped with relief.

"Can you tell where she went from here?" said Polly eagerly.

"Should we really keep tracking her? If she's strong enough to break a fence, she's not in immediate danger." Bethany put her hand on Polly's arm, hoping to talk sense into her friend.

"I half-expected us to find her collapsed in the orchard and thought we'd have to carry her back to Polly's," said Brittany.

"Alya, what do you think?" Polly asked as the hunter's daughter examined the ground carefully.

"If I didn't know there was a town to the east, I'd follow the orchard west to the lake. The trail is more well-traveled in that direction," Bethany volunteered as Alya's examination continued.

"She could be up in the hills or squatting in someone's summer cabin. That's where I'd go if I wanted to hide and not run into people." Brittany lifted her arm and pointed to the crest of the hill.

"Guys, I think there's something else going on here." Alya kneeled down on all fours. She seemed to be double-checking the earth.

"Okay, Sarah Connor, what's up?" Brittany had her hands on her hips. Polly felt nervous energy pulsing through the whole group.

"Don't freak out, but there are other tracks here—animal tracks. Bear, I think. Unless this is the world's biggest cougar." Alya peered at another print. "Oh yeah, here's the back paw. Definitely bear. They go east, toward town. It was probably looking for garbage and paused to sniff through the fence."

"Uh, what's this?" Bethany pulled a tuft of brown fur from the gap in the fence, much lower down than where they found the white hair.

Alya looked at the fur and sighed. "Pretty sure that's bear fur. If it had just been sniffing, I doubt it would have shoved against the fence that hard. It might have nothing to do with the girl, though. If they'd made contact and it went bad, this place would be a mess."

A rustling in the orchard caught the group's attention. And then a scream.

"Oh my god! Oh my god!" Caroline put her face in her hands.

"Was that the wind?" asked Bethany.

"Maybe, but—"

Rrrrrr-uuuu-aaar! A gruff animal grunt cut Brittany off.

"Yup . . .that's a bear." Alya's voice was nervous and certain.

"EEEEEEEEEEE!"

The girls all recognized the scream from their first encounter with the albino fugitive.

"Oh my god, she's getting attacked RIGHT NOW!" Caroline waved her hands uselessly.

"What are the chances she could survive a fight with a bear?" Polly asked. Adrenaline coursed through her.

KRACK!

A tuft of leaves puffed up above the northwest end of the orchard.

"Help! Please! Someone HELP!" a girl cried from far away.

"That has to be her. Hurry, there isn't time!" Polly started running in the direction of the leaf cloud.

Chapter 10

Sy'kai ran along a border of trees, heading west in a ditch that separated the south side of the orchard from the fenced-in homes on her left. She felt the sun warming her back in spite of the chilly air. She stopped to walk once she sensed that the danger was far enough behind.

The brown pants she'd taken were thick and ribbed, and they made an annoying *brrrp-rrrr-brrrp-rrrr* sound with each stride. Eventually the sound grew on her, and she felt her spirit lift. A black bird over a body of water decorated the soft cream sweater. Sy'kai lifted the fabric in an attempt to identify the inverted image. The word "loon" leapt to her mind. She smiled again. Her new mental image of an elegant bird musically coasting across calm water was soothing. She hugged herself.

I wonder where the nearest shelter is. Something better than that old shack in the orchard. I can smell fresh water not far away. Maybe that is my best option. There will be structures near there, I am certain. Only I cannot risk drawing Nur-gahl to the dwellings of these beings, however ignorant and selfish they are. The young females I saw . . . I felt concern from a few of them. But so much fear! They reeked of it.

A warm yellow sun crept upward into a clear blue sky while Sy'kai walked. As she crested the hill, she saw a placid lake inlaid on the valley floor below. She inhaled deeply as she reached the bottom of the hill, savoring the subtle vapor full of mineral-rich water. Sy'kai scanned the pathways and buildings that stretched in both directions, out of sight from everything she'd left behind.

Some of these dwellings are void of life; I can hear it. Some have been empty for a long time. That will do nicely. If I select one far from the others, it will be safe enough to wait out the remainder of my healing process. In the unhappy event that Nur-gahl discovers me again, our battle will be of little danger to others. I cannot be certain, but I can hope. I will gather some food before I go down.

Sunlight glinted off something on the ground ahead and Sy'kai ran into the orchard to claim it, full of hunger and confused by the object's sudden appeal. A small round reddish-brown piece of metal reflected a bright beam into her eyes. She plucked it off the ground and instinctively swallowed it.

A shiver slid up her backbone and spread throughout her body, waking every cell in a wave of contentment that crystallized beneath her skin. Tingling needled at the wound in her arm, and she pushed up her sleeve in time to watch the wound heal and push out the thread she had carefully sewn through her flesh. The stained brown thread fell to the earth and tumbled along the ground until a tuft of grass caught it.

I am healed? How is this possible? What was that substance? Oh, why did I not stop to examine it before giving in to hunger? It had markings and writing on it. And it smelled of blood. I hope I will know that metal again. I should save it if I am lucky enough to find more—I may have need of such healing before my war is won.

Mottled gray feathers lifted off the ground like bashful fingers from the base of a cherry tree a few feet ahead. A heartbeat later, Sy'kai could tell that the animal to whom the feathers belonged was already dead. A swell of sorrow at the loss of life filled her even though she had no connection to the bird. She closed the distance gracefully and bent to touch it.

Sy'kai stroked the dead bird gently, pouring remorse through her fingertips. Mental pictures of other feathered creatures from a multitude of worlds—some memories, some archived knowledge—popped into her head one after another until she felt a tear push its way down her cheek.

Cold air kissed her fingertips and her muscles contracted. She fought the urge to pull away, badly wanting to somehow comfort the bird. She stroked its feathers again and the dead body quivered. Sy'kai drew her hand back, but regained her courage and gently lifted the limp bird, cradling it in her open palms. She brought the body up to her face and looked closely at the thousands of lines throughout its feathers. She drew a breath and slowly let the heat from her lungs fill the air around the bird.

Another rattle of movement roused the bird and it hopped up, standing on her hand as though it had just landed. The bird cocked its reanimated head and inspected her thoughtfully through beady black eyes. It puffed the orange-red feathers of its chest, let out a fierce squeak, and flapped away.

Sy'kai watched until the bird landed on a branch. A shaft of yellow light darted past the bird, through the rustling leaves. She raised her forearm to shield her eyes and heard the unmistakable *RUMPF* of a bear's snarl.

It was already too late.

A giant black-clawed paw slammed into the side of her head. She flew sideways and hit the dirt with a painful thud.

"You thought to HIDE? From ME? Ha!" Guttural grunts came out of the bear in a spiteful deep voice. "Out smart me? No!"

Sy'kai gripped her head to stop the pain. She dug her foot into the ground and pushed herself away. The bear sauntered forward and swiped at her again, sending her up into the air. Agony ripped into her back. A tree trunk caught her belly, knocking the breath from her chest.

"ME, Nur-gahl! I am wrath. And POWER!" The bear let out another roar.

Nur-gahl waited while Sy'kai struggled to stand. He paced back and forth, pausing to take one step forward and one back, mustering the patience he needed to wait for his prey to compose herself. He shook his head and clarity swept over his glassy eyes.

"You are no match for me in this shape, Sy'kai. You should have held your original shift as well; that one had magic of its own! This form might cloud my thoughts, but I can retain it as long as I want. I have waited patiently for your full transformation. Now I will destroy you utterly and obtain your gifts. Comply and your death shall be swift. Resist and I will make your final days an endless nightmare."

"How is it you have your full strength already, old foe? I hardly remember you, or myself." Sy'kai propped herself up against a tree. Her back screamed with the pain of her open wounds, but she forced her body to stay upright.

"Idiot brat. Remember yourself! I cannot open my own fissures in spacetime. I have no need, not when I can follow you, letting your reckless body shoulder the burden."

Sy'kai summoned all her energy to reach into Nur-gahl's head. She desperately probed for information. A giant mouth with hundreds of razor-sharp steel teeth accosted her vision. The scene shifted then to the girls Sy'kai had seen the night before. She watched in horror as Nur-gahl's mouth moved from girl to girl, leaving nothing behind.

"You do not need my gifts to feed. Why wait for me?"

"Because, insolent wretch, I owe our mother vengeance. Your betrayal will be answered. I will not allow your escape."

"My escape?" A surge of indignant rage overtook Sy'kai. She still remembered so little of Nur-gahl, or of her home and past. But he must not be allowed to roam free. "You are the one who will pay!"

Sy'kai lunged forward, arms outstretched, funneling all her rage and pain toward Nur-gahl. A shock wave of telekinetic energy blasted the bear straight through the tree behind him. Sy'kai cried out for help then, using the last of her consciousness to guide the broken cherry tree trunk back and on top of the bear, pinning him to the ground.

Chapter 11

Polly heard panting and the thumping of footfalls behind her. She kept her eye on the spot in the orchard where she'd seen the leaf explosion, where she thought the albino girl's cry had come from. As much as Polly wanted to help the strange girl, she *needed* to know what a naked girl had been doing at the site of an electrical storm. Something gave Polly the chills—prickles danced up her spine as she got closer.

She reached a gap in the trees and found the pale girl there, collapsed on the orchard floor, clothed but barefoot. Her cream sweater was slashed along the back, caked with dirt and blood. Clumps of brown fur were trapped under the trunk of a fallen tree across from where the girl lay. Polly kneeled by the unconscious body as her friends skidded to a halt behind her.

"Hello? Miss?" Polly said. "Help is here." She waited, but the girl remained motionless.

"Is she still alive?" Alya asked hopefully.

Polly glanced back. "It's hard to tell."

"I don't think we should move her. Lean in and listen for breathing." Bethany stepped forward. Brittany moved around to the other side of the albino girl. "We need to check for a pulse."

Polly carefully lifted a tangled lock of hair from the girl's face and bent forward, within an inch of her smooth ivory skin. Ragged faint breaths puffed from the girl's lips. Polly felt the chain around her neck slide forward and brush the girl's cheek.

Her eyes popped open, wild and ice-blue. She sat up and snatched the chain off Polly's neck, shoveling it into her mouth like a starving feral child.

"What the hell!" Brittany said, jumping. Polly stumbled back. Caroline and Alya gasped in unison.

"Are you . . . okay?" Polly's adrenaline slammed her heart up and down.

The albino girl closed her eyes and a blue-green glow emanated from the slashes on her back. Polly and her friends watched in awe as the wounds beneath the stained fabric shrank and disappeared. The girl's eyelids popped wide again.

"Oh my GOD!" Caroline gripped Alya's sleeve.

"I am healed. Thank you for that." Her eyeballs rolled back for a moment. The rest of the group watched in shock as the pale girl shivered, head tilted to the sky. She stopped suddenly and composed herself. "Copper! Yes, thank you for the copper."

"Who *are* you?" Alya asked, stepping forward. Caroline slipped squarely behind Alya.

"My name? I am Sy'kai. I am not from your world. I have lost my memory temporarily, although I now have much of the knowledge I need to function here. I have sensed you all following me. I prefer not to interfere with alien life forms, particularly civilized ones, but I can feel that you want to help. I may need you." Sy'kai rose and stretched.

"No shit, you're not from around here!" Brittany said, observing Sy'kai's porcelain face.

"Where are you from? Are you an alien? An angel?" Bethany took a step toward Sy'kai, who replied with a stony, deadpan expression.

"What happened to the thing that attacked you? Was it a bear?" Polly's gaze darted around, her awareness expanding to the rest of the orchard.

"Nur-gahl." Sy'kai nodded knowingly and prodded at a large tuft of fur caught in the broken tree trunk.

"Um, what?" said Alya.

"Do you mind?" Bethany reached toward one of Sy'kai's ice-blue eyes, and the girl gave a slight nod of consent. Bethany gently lifted her patient's eyelid. "Her pupils aren't overly dilated—I think we can rule out drug use."

"You're not actually a real nurse." Alya rolled her eyes.

"She's a damn sight closer than any of us," Polly glowered, grateful that the twins knew anything about medicine.

"Never mind that. What's a Nurr Gull?" asked Caroline.

"Nur-gahl. He is a dangerous creature, pursuing me for . . .vengeance, it seems." Sy'kai helped herself to Polly's backpack. She fished out a muffin, sniffed it, and took a bite. She smiled, chewed, and swallowed. "I was trying to lead him away from your homes. I had hoped to hide from him until my full strength and memories return."

"Why is your memory gone?" said Polly.

"I was not sure at first—I thought it was a side effect of my transition to this form. However, if I am to believe Nur-gahl, opening a fissure in spacetime disrupts one's neurological functions."

Polly's eyebrows arched. Caroline's mouth formed an O.

"Well now, that makes perfect sense, doesn't it?" Alya crossed her arms.

"Your wounds have closed, but you should still come with us to a hospital," said Bethany. Brittany tapped the side of her forehead and moved her finger in a circle.

"I am not insane, my friend." Sy'kai gave Brittany a blank look. "Your caregivers should not be allowed to examine me. I will be detained. I can see that in your mind, and in your sister's."

"Um, Sai-kee . . . sorry if I mispronounced that. But maybe you *need* to be detained. To get better. For a little while," Caroline said, stepping out from behind Alya.

"We just want to help. Nobody is going to lock you up." Polly raised her hands submissively as she spoke.

Sy'kai laid her hand on Polly's chest and closed her eyes. "So much pain. Fear and heartache taint your every thought." Sy'kai opened her vivid eyes, which bored into Polly's. A soothing warmth rushed from Sy'kai's core into Polly, washing over her like humidity in a summer meadow. Polly saw a flash of nebula as her mind's eye overtook her waking field of vision. She sucked in a breath at the raw beauty of it. Pressure washed over Polly's body for an instant and her muscles relaxed. Polly felt as though her body floated up off the ground. For a moment, she wondered if she would continue soaring up into the atmosphere and off into space, to wherever Sy'kai's stars waited for her. Serenity invaded Polly's mind with splashes of light and pushed away the sorrow that had forged such deep roots. Polly felt freer than she had ever thought possible. She looked down to see her feet still on the ground.

"What was that?"

"A cleansing. I'm sorry, but the effects will not be permanent."

Polly felt too at peace to care.

"Okay, so no hospital then?" said Brittany. She cocked an eyebrow.

"No medical treatment is necessary," Sy'kai said calmly.

"What are you saying? That we should just leave you here?" said Bethany.

"Let's not forget about the bear that might still be around here somewhere. We're better off indoors, behind locks and strong walls," said Alya. She slipped her bangles back on her wrist.

"Come back to my place, Sy'kai, and we'll figure out what to do." Polly lifted her backpack. She nodded in the general direction of home and set off, leading the way.

"That is a really strange name. Where are you from again?" Caroline's pitch escalated as she walked.

"Let's give you a name from this world, for now," Polly said, looking back at Sy'kai. "We'll call you Psyche. It means 'spirit.' In Greek mythology, Psyche was a beautiful woman married to the god of love." Polly flashed a smile, which Sy'kai returned with awkward mirror-like precision.

"Greek mythology? Wow, you *did* just get your brain scrambled," Brittany said to Polly.

"I like it. Good, then. Call me Psyche."

"Sounds pretty nice to me," Caroline said softly.

"How long do you think you'll need before your memory returns?" Alya looked between Psyche and Polly. "I hate to be a wet blanket, but Polly already has one sick person resting at home."

"As I said, I am not ill. But I also do not know how long it will take for my brain and this new body to adjust to this plane."

Alya took a deep breath and decided to leave the conversation there.

An idea struck Polly like a slap in the face. If Psyche had some kind of alien ability to heal, perhaps they were destined to meet. She wondered if any of the other girls, including the mind-reading traveler herself, had picked up on the idea as well.

"Mom should be in better shape by the time we get home." A *crack-snap* from far off in the cherry trees startled them.

"Was that . . .?" Polly froze, and the rest followed suit.

"Could be," said Alya.

"Let's pick up the pace then." Bethany shooed the group forward.

CA-RACK! The noise was louder and closer. Caroline darted forward, sprinting ahead now. The girls jogged to catch up.

"How fast can a bear move?" Polly asked Alya as they ran.

"Faster than we can, so you better hope we're almost home," said Alya.

"Maybe that wasn't the bear. Maybe he's not coming this way." Bethany didn't sound convincing, even to herself.

"And maybe teenage girls make great snacks," said Brittany as the tree line opened in front of them to reveal the side of Polly's house.

Chapter 12

The group tumbled into Polly's kitchen through the sliding glass door, which they'd left open.

"Shhhhhhh!" hissed Polly. She rolled the door shut as soon as everyone was through.

"Polly? Girls?" her mom called from the living room.

Polly's head whipped around at Psyche. The girl was unfit to be seen, not without getting roped into that hospital visit she didn't want. As though listening to Polly's thoughts, Psyche crept backward.

"Quick. Put this on." Polly peeled off her windbreaker and shoved it at Psyche.

"And tie your hair back." Bethany handed a lace scrunchie to the startled girl.

"Where on Earth did you wander off to all by yourselves?" Polly's mom stood at the archway connecting the kitchen to the living room.

"You look better, Mrs. Michaels," Caroline offered brightly. Polly felt her cheeks flush.

"And who is this?" Polly's mom looked at Psyche with gentle curiosity. Her expression turned to puzzlement as she noticed the leaves in Psyche's hair.

"The new girl at school," Polly blurted. "She lives down on Lakeview Road, so we went to meet her. It was faster to cut through the orchard."

"Polly, you know they consider it trespassing to walk through Lakeview Hills. I wouldn't put it past one of those old men to take a shot at someone out among their precious cherry trees. Please, girls, for my fragile nerves, stay out of the orchard."

Psyche opened her mouth to speak but looked at Polly for approval. The latter glared and offered a curt head shake.

"Yes, Ma'am," said Bethany and Brittany in unison.

"Don't worry, we won't be going back," Alya said with total certainty. Caroline nodded her vigorous agreement.

"And your friend? What's your name, dear?" Mom said to Psyche.

"They told me my name is hard to pronounce, so I'm Psyche now." Her voice had a melodic quality Polly hadn't noticed before.

"Okay." Polly's mom gave her daughter a disapproving frown and looked to the others in turn. "It's Psyche, for now. But Polly, I'd like you to learn how to say your friend's real name properly." Polly's mom slung her purse over her shoulder. "I'm going into town for a few hours. I have a follow-up appointment at the hospital. And I'm going to check in at the boutique. If I don't keep in touch with Stephanie, I'm worried she'll give my job away permanently."

Polly's mom grinned at the group. One by one they returned furtive looks riddled with impatient energy. Polly's mom eyed each girl, her gaze resting questioningly on her daughter.

"Um, you're parked in the garage, right?" Polly's pulse quickened as she visualized her mom walking down the driveway with a huge bear looking on.

"Yes, why?" Her mom's eyes narrowed.

"No reason. Just thinking about safety. Always better to keep the car inside." Polly shoved her hands in her pockets and looked away.

"Say hi to our parents if you see them," chirped Bethany. Brittany rolled her eyes.

"I sure will, girls. All of you, be good while I'm gone. Watch a little television or something. I probably won't be home for dinner, so order a pizza." Polly's mom smiled. And with a click of the door, she was gone.

"So, what should we *really* do?" asked Alya.

"Make sure the doors are locked for a start," said Bethany, peering out the sliding glass door and into the orchard.

"Why don't we just watch TV like your mom said?" Caroline looked like she needed a mundane moment.

"Chilling out would give Psyche a chance to rest," said Polly.

"And remember," Psyche added.

"Works for me." Brittany plucked an apple off the kitchen counter and turned the corner.

The Michaels' living room was the nicest room in the house. Polly's mom had fallen in love with the renovated little farmhouse entirely because of that central space. As in the kitchen, the high ceiling rose to the second floor, but on the living room side, the sloping roof was higher still—easily twenty feet. A skylight brightened the cream-painted walls. Bare cedar beams gave off the slightest hint of scent, which mingled with the mustiness that wafted up from the basement.

"Let's see what Saturday afternoon TV has to offer out here in the sticks. Do you even get a music channel?" Bethany pushed a red button with chrome trim on the large wood frame picture tube set against the far wall.

"We get regular cable, just like in town." Polly rolled her eyes.

"Why don't you try channel ten? There might be something on the news about that storm," said Caroline.

Bethany's mouth twisted. She tilted her head, weighing options as she changed the channel. "Or we could look for music videos. I could use a little Madonna to lighten the mood."

"Don't be silly; the news is a good idea. That might jog Psyche's memory," Alya said as she reached past the twins to turn the dial again.

"I doubt it's that simple." Polly's eyes were full of sympathy as she looked to Psyche's frown. She followed the girl's strange ice-blue gaze to the television. On screen, a man in a trench coat was standing next to a destroyed tree. It was unmistakably the Lakeview Hills orchard.

"—and the fire department is quite certain this damage was not caused by the mysterious electrical storm two nights ago. The fire chief declined to speculate, but the owners of the Lakeview Hills Cherry Orchard have theories ranging from vandalism to a wild animal attack. A small amount of blood was found at the scene, and we've been told police are investigating, although no victim or victims have been located."

"Whoa, that was fast!" Brittany said before slapping her hand over her mouth.

"I told you, it's not that remote out here. Obviously, people down on Lakeview Road heard that tree snap and somebody called the cops. They know something's going on." Polly's sense of vindication was quickly replaced by concern.

"It is very unfortunate that your security people will be looking for me. I cannot let them learn from studying me. There is simply no time." Psyche's brow furrowed.

"No, they're not looking for you, specifically. We won't let anyone catch you. They just . . . when you ran away from us the other night, I had to do something." Polly wrung her hands, full of regret. She pushed the image of Psyche handcuffed to a bed out of her mind, but from the look of terror etched in those ceramic-smooth features, it was too late.

"Psyche, did you just read my mind? Is that really what's happening here?"

"I knew it!" blurted Brittany.

"This is truly incredible," said Bethany.

Each of Polly's friends looked at Psyche with wide, curious eyes.

"Psyche, I know you need information, but I think you should stay out of our heads as much as possible," Polly said firmly. She sighed, adding, "You're right that we want to help. And we'll tell you anything you need to know. We're trying to keep you safe."

"She is safe. We all are, so let's not panic," said Caroline calmly. "Polly's mom is the only person who's seen Psyche, right?"

The girls all turned to Psyche for confirmation.

"I did have an encounter with a man and a woman. The place where I found these clothes. I hid there. The man called me a thief and drew a weapon. It was a long metal tube and I sensed it could kill me."

"Sounds like a gun," said Bethany.

"Fantastic." Alya buried her face in her hands.

"It won't be long before the police make that connection. That incident probably explains the siren we heard," said Brittany.

"So, what do we do, just stay hidden, hoping her memory comes back?" said Alya.

"If she's wanted for a crime, we could get in trouble, too." Caroline looked at everyone but Psyche.

"I do not wish to be a problem." Psyche stood up and took off Polly's jacket.

"Keep the jacket. In fact, come up to my room and we'll get you some real clothes. You're not much bigger than me. And Mom might have some old stuff you can wear."

"Why don't I order that pizza while you're upstairs? One pepperoni and one vegetarian? Good for everyone?" Bethany said, pointing at each girl in turn.

"As long as you order from Antonio's, I don't care what you get," said Alya.

"It's gotta be Domino's to get delivery out here," Polly called over her shoulder as she escorted Psyche upstairs to her bedroom.

"This is my room," she said. "The one down the hall is Mom's. The bathroom is across the hall. You use a bathroom, right?" Psyche answered with a cocked head, so Polly changed the subject. "Let's get you into something warm and comfortable. Do you wear a bra? No, silly question." Polly drew a pair of worn jeans from her dresser drawer and took a plaid shirt off a hanger in her closet. "Okay, here you go. You'll fit right in wearing this stuff. Then again, there's no disguising this ultra-pale thing you've got going on."

"Sorry, Polly. I feel bad that I am an inconvenience. And an embarrassment."

"No, Psyche, you're no trouble at all! You need a hand right now. I just want to help." Polly paused and looked at her Lite-Brite. The plastic box rested face-up on the floor just as she'd left it. The unicorn scene was so densely packed with pegs, none of it had dislodged despite being knocked to the ground. The lightless pegs bore no resemblance to the luminous creature in her memory. Polly turned back to find Psyche examining her intently.

"You want to help me because you cannot help your mother. I understand. I wish I could help her myself."

"Wait, what? Why can't you help my mom? You healed yourself by *eating* my necklace! I've got more copper in a change dish downstairs. And I could get my hands on a lot more, I'm sure. Can't you channel that into more healing power, or energy or life-force or whatever?"

"Honestly, Polly, I do not know. There is so much about my life—about who I am and what I am that I still do not remember. For example, I can hear thoughts of those nearby, which you have already noticed. But I also believe I can move things with my mind. I believe I can listen to thoughts farther away, if I concentrate. Yet I am unsure if these feelings are true, and if so, how these abilities work."

"Well, let's just get you back to normal, whatever that is for you—sooner rather than later. Mom could be running out of time. And I want you to have all your abilities, whatever they are, back in fighting shape." Polly pushed past Psyche. "I'll leave you to change."

Polly found her friends downstairs watching an episode of *Unsolved Mysteries*. Robert Stack's ominous voice always sent subtle prickles up Polly's neck. Then the distraction wore off and rage swelled in her belly. Why should she stick her neck out for this girl, this creature, if she wouldn't even *try* to heal Mom? What had drawn her into Psyche's drama in the first place? Maybe it was a misplaced need to fix something broken. Polly forced herself to look only between her friends and the TV, and not at Psyche's lost-puppy face.

Chingling-tinkling. Crack. SMASH.

"What was that?" snapped Alya.

"Where's Psyche?" asked Bethany.

Polly ran to the kitchen. Psyche had collapsed on the floor like a rag doll. One of her hands pinched the palm of the other. The small ceramic bowl containing her mom's loose change was cracked in pieces on the slate tiles. Nickels and dimes lay scattered about. All the pennies were gone.

Psyche twitched a moment, hands still clasped, then lay still. Her eyelids fluttered.

Chapter 13

Psyche slept soundly. Bethany and Brittany checked her pulse and temperature, but refrained from confident declarations. Polly and Alya carried Psyche to the living room couch.

"Is it just me, or does she seem … normal?" Alya said as she gently released Psyche's upper body onto a couch cushion.

"Define normal," said Polly.

"The muscles in her arms. The bones underneath. The weight of her body. It all feels like she's a regular human being. Shouldn't we still be considering the possibility that she's not mentally well? And we're being taken for a ride?"

"When you look at her now," Polly gestured at the sleeping girl, "yeah, she does seem normal. But every time you think about that, remember the things we've seen her do. Like eating my necklace and slashes glowing until they healed on her back. I don't know about you, but I'm going to remember that for the rest of my life."

"I still say it could be some kind of science experiment." Alya looked away, out the window into the sky.

"And if you're right about that, do we dump her on the road to fend for herself?" Bethany said as she stepped back to Polly's side.

"Of course not," Alya said quietly as she sat down.

"How long should we let her sleep?" Caroline asked the twins.

"I'm not sure. We just know what we've picked up from Mom and Dad. Alya was right—we're not experts," said Bethany.

"That's putting it mildly." Alya crossed her arms.

"Hey, if you can do better." Brittany frowned at Alya, who looked apologetic.

"Even if they were nurses, we're not talking about a human girl. We don't know what she is yet, but we have to trust that if consuming copper helps her, then it's something her body is meant to process naturally." Polly kneeled down next to Psyche.

Psyche's flawless skin reminded Polly of a marble statue. Her angelic eyelashes were motionless. Only her sculpted lips held the palest tint of pink. Polly untied Psyche's ponytail and returned the scrunchie to Bethany, who in turn placed it on the coffee table like a used tissue. Once spread out, Psyche's platinum hair betrayed the truth of her wild adventure, still tangled with leaves and twigs. After sizing Psyche up for a long moment, Polly grew more certain that the girl would be able to heal someone other than herself if given the chance.

"When she wakes up, do you think she'll do some cool alien tricks?" Brittany stood next to the couch, peering down on Psyche's face from above.

"What makes her an alien?" Bethany fired at her sister.

"She could be a bizarre natural mutation." Caroline gazed thoughtfully at Psyche.

"I don't think it matters what we call her. When Psyche put her hand on my chest back in the orchard, I felt her energy travel into me. I can't explain it. We won't know more until her amnesia wears off." Polly carefully laid a thin knit blanket over Psyche and retreated to a nearby armchair.

"Am I the only one thinking that she might be able to help your mom? Do some alien voodoo on the cancer?" Brittany spoke quietly, but it was enough to unnerve the whole room.

"I already asked her—upstairs, when I gave her those clothes. She said no." Polly's voice faded to a whisper.

Psyche's eyelids snapped open. The girls collectively gasped. Polly leaped up.

"I told you," Psyche said, "that I did not know. My memory is back now, and I can speak with more specificity." She sat up.

"Are you feeling better?" asked Caroline.

"Forget that, let her finish," said Alya.

Psyche's gaze drifted from girl to girl, coming to rest on Polly's eager face. Polly leaned forward, waiting for more.

"It *is* possible for me to transfer enough life force to another being to repair tissue and damaged cells; however, in a corporeal body, like this or any other form I take in your realm, I will need a substantial initial charge. A large quantity of the most conductive element on this planet will be required." Psyche pointed at the shiny Sanskrit Om character around Alya's neck.

"Silver? I'm sure we can find something you can use. Other than my necklace." Alya rolled her hair into a bun while her bracelets jingled.

"Yeah, I think we have some silver around the house. How much do you need?" Polly didn't break eye contact with Psyche.

"It is difficult to say. Perhaps something of this weight." Psyche picked up a soapstone wolf sculpture from the side table next to the couch. Bethany held out her hand and Psyche transferred the object to her.

"This thing must weigh a whole pound. At least." Bethany raised and lowered the wolf, trying to guess its mass.

"Uhhhhh, how much does silver weigh? How many little pendants are you going to need to get to a *pound*?" Brittany's eyes narrowed as she looked from the stone wolf to the pendant around Alya's neck.

"Shhhh . . ." Bethany frowned.

"Who's going to hear? And it's a good thing we're isolated if we need to plan for stealing jewelry. This isn't rocket science. A pound is a lot when it comes to jewelry!" Brittany glared at her sister.

"We can't steal jewelry or silver or *anything!*" blurted Caroline, leaping to her feet. "We can't *steal* from anyone. I can't! I won't!"

"Calm down, Caroline. Nobody's going to make you do anything." Polly resolved in that moment to get the silver any way she could. As quickly as she could manage.

"My friends, please, do not argue. I would help your mother, even if the risk to me is great. But have you all forgotten about Nur-gahl? I can see why you might; none of you have encountered him, not properly. Whether he remains a bear or takes another form, he will be a danger to everyone and everything in your world unless I stop him. He has come here to feed, to propagate himself, and to murder me. I do not think I can destroy him in one pass. Instead, I must draw him out of this dimensional plane and into another. Until that goal is achieved, I cannot afford to focus on the maintenance of a single life."

"Psyche, we could just let the local cops and game officers track that bear. If you've got some healing gift, don't you think you could at least give it a shot? Polly's been pretty good about helping *you* so far," said Alya.

"To you, I sound ridiculous. And you are right to question everything I have said."

"Maybe she *can* read minds." Alya turned to the twins.

"Again, I do want to help. But I cannot stress enough the seriousness—and the truth—of everything I have told you." Psyche's posture went rigid.

"You mentioned something about Nur-gahl hunting you for vengeance. I'm assuming you're the same . . . species. What could you possibly have done to that monster?" Polly forced her best poker face while her heart raced.

Psyche flushed. "There was a conflict in our temple. I cannot explain it in a way that would make sense to beings that live such short lives trapped in flesh." Psyche said the last word with disdain, and it finally occurred to Polly that her guest was uncomfortable—in more ways than they realized.

"Okay, tell us again: How do we handle this . . . not-really-a-bear scary mutant thing?" said Bethany.

"I have been traveling from one planet to another, often crossing a dimensional barrier, drawn to sentient life wherever and however it exists. Each time I slice through spacetime, my essence is scrambled. Still, I have no choice. In his mind, neither does Nur-gahl. He is a worthy adversary, and while my victory over him is not certain I must still try. That is my burden and my fate."

"You're right—this chick has lost it," Brittany said to Alya.

"Be fair, we've all seen some strange things the last two days. There's something going on here, even if she does need some kind of psychological help." Caroline sat next to Psyche on the couch.

Caroline reached into her backpack and pulled out a brush, gesturing to Psyche for permission to detangle her hair. Psyche nodded and kneeled on the floor in front of Caroline.

"If I am successful in defeating Nur-gahl, I will return here and undertake the healing of Polly's mother."

Polly relaxed back in her chair. The girls watched as Caroline timidly brushed all the debris from Psyche's hair, working her way up until she had a three-foot sash of satin that shone like pearls spun into thread. Psyche stopped Caroline's hand with a soft touch and held her gaze. She reached out to Caroline then as she had to Polly, placing her palm on Caroline's forehead, gripping it carefully with fingers spread. Caroline looked tense and slightly startled, but a heartbeat later, her features slackened. Her eyelids grew heavy and fell shut. Psyche released Caroline's head, smoothing her hand down her straight black hair, supporting Caroline's shoulder to keep her relaxed body from falling over.

"I feel . . . great!" Caroline opened her eyes and smiled.

"Was that the same thing you did to me?" Polly cocked her head to one side, noting Caroline's easy smile.

"Not exactly the same. Anxiety and anguish inhabit your souls in different ways."

"What are we supposed to make of that? I can't speak for all of us, but personally, I'm going to need some of this stuff to start making sense. *Real* sense." Alya gripped her hips and squared her stance.

"I promise you will understand. In time." Psyche looked to the front door in anticipation. Moments later, there was a knock.

Chapter 14

None of the girls made a move. There was another knock. Polly and Psyche froze like statues.

"Who is that?" Polly gripped the arms of her chair.

"Pizza, remember?" Brittany held an open palm to Bethany, who produced a wallet. Polly relaxed back in her chair.

Minutes later, the girls were eating in silence, the fresh, hot aroma of bread, cheese, herbs, and roasted vegetables filling the large room.

"Thank you for sharing your nourishment with me." Psyche's authenticity and melodic voice compensated for her awkward word choices. The girls were growing used to their odd guest. All smiled in return.

"Well, we took you in; you're our responsibility now," said Bethany, with a wink and a hint of sarcasm that flew over Psyche like snow in the wind.

"I do not wish to be a burden. I can sustain myself and hunt Nur-gahl alone."

"We can help with sustenance, but I don't know about the hunting part. Not even with this one on board." Brittany hooked her thumb at Alya.

"Hey, I can track a bear! It's the killing part that's got me worried." Alya sat forward, a slice of pizza drooping off her hand. "We've still got that bear spray. I think we can help Psyche find this thing. There has to be a way we can back her up."

"No way! We're kids! We're not hunters *or* nurses!" Caroline blurted at Alya and the twins. "We're not social workers or saints either!" she fired at Polly.

Even Bethany looked startled at Caroline's outburst. "Take it easy. Nobody is going to make you march off to battle."

Polly stood up and paced back and forth for a moment. "All things considered, I think we can help. Psyche is powerful. With a little back-up, maybe she can kill it, not just lead it off somewhere. And when we're done, I and I alone will steal the silver she needs to cure Mom. If I have to hit all the jewelry stores and pawn shops in town, I don't care. I don't want any help either. It's my mom, so I'll take the risk." Polly gave Psyche a hard stare, adding, "But you don't leave this world until you've cured Mom. That part is a deal breaker. Maybe you don't absolutely need us. Then again, maybe you do. Maybe having our help makes all the difference between you killing *him* and him killing *you.*"

Silence crushed the room.

Polly's mind drifted to a future in which Nur-gahl had the freedom to kill at will, roaming far beyond Bella Vista, carving into buildings and crowds with giant bolts of red-hot current. He was no longer a bear, but a huge beast covered in coarse hair and scales. A legion of similarly horrible creatures hissed and roared behind him. Polly suddenly wondered if this vision was her own imagination or if it came from Psyche.

The phone rang then and the girls flinched in unison. Polly marched around the corner and picked up the receiver.

"Michaels residence . . . Hi, Mom . . . Sure, that's no problem, we'll be fine. I'll ask some of the girls to sleep over again. I won't be here on my own." Polly hung up and returned to the living room. "That was Mom. One of the doctors wants to put her on an IV overnight to rehydrate her. I guess she's been scary sick, even for a chemo patient."

"Polly, I'm so sorry." Alya gave Polly an uncharacteristic hug. Emotion churned in Polly's stomach, but she didn't fight the embrace.

"I have one more thing to share with you." Psyche stood, set her pizza carefully on the coffee table, and held out her arm. "I am now able to draw information more quickly from the recesses of my mind, as well as the collective knowledge of your world."

"Uh, how's that?" Brittany looked fascinated as she examined Psyche's palm.

"When I travel from one plane of existence to another, my corporeal body and any possessions are left behind. But when I take a new shape—generally the most viable life form mentally projected near my location—my physical structure includes a knowledge retrieval gland. In this body, I am able to activate it in the fleshy part of my right appendage."

"So, you have some kind of gadget in your palm?" Bethany curled loose tendrils of hair behind her ears and joined her sister in examining Psyche's hand.

"While my knowledge retrieval is still underway, there is a side effect—I become violently ill or lose consciousness. I had hoped consuming some copper in your kitchen would offset the reaction earlier, but I was wrong."

"Are you saying your 'knowledge retrieval' is complete? And you want to do that trance thing again?" Polly shoved the sleeves of her sweatshirt up to her elbows, getting ready for a mess.

"Short of exploring the surrounding land in hopes of locating and battling Nur-gahl, I can think of no other way to make progress. Do not be alarmed, I am in no danger." And without another word, Psyche pinched the center of her right hand and collapsed back onto the couch. Her body jerked a few times, and then she came to, groggy but able to sit on her own.

"I still need more practice manipulating the gland in my human body. I have more knowledge now, but not of Nur-gahl or his whereabouts."

"What did you learn just then?" said Alya. Her skepticism seemed to be melting away.

"I can offer you a clearer explanation, in your language, of what, exactly, I am."

"Ooooo, this should be intense!" Brittany took a mouthful of pizza without looking away. Polly eyed Brittany before turning her attention to Psyche.

"The realm I come from exists inside what you would call an 'interstellar dust cloud'—a nebula. There is no rock and matter foundation where we live. We are beings of pure energy. To visit temporally and gravitationally restricted physical worlds, my essence experiences an accelerated morpho-genetic transformation after passing through a fissure in spacetime." Psyche's deadpan expression passed from Polly to Alya, and then around the room until she reached her host again.

"Okay, I realize you're using English, but that information is not exactly 'my language,' or anything resembling what we know." Polly looked to her friends for confirmation and received only blank stares in return.

BANG—KA-BANG.

Just then, a catastrophic crash from the kitchen sent a tremor of terror through the house.

Polly jumped to her feet and ran to the kitchen doorway. "Oh, god, what the—" Her gaze darted to the sliding glass door. "Something's running away. Wait, no, it's coming back! HOLY SHIT, IT'S THE BEAR!"

A mountain of greasy dark brown fur thundered at Polly with impossible speed. Panic nailed her feet to the ground. She locked eyes with the animal. Ghastly bloodshot pupils oozed pus down the bear's face, coating its muzzle with mucus that sprayed as Nur-gahl roared. Psyche slid past Polly like a petal in a summer breeze. She stared down the bear as though it were nothing more than a small dog yapping and snapping on the other side of the too-thin glass.

"You dishonor yourself by feeding off fear," Psyche said to the beast. "Every morsel you take is a stain on your essence." She spoke at little more than a whisper, but the bear still stopped to meet her frosty eyes.

Psyche's hard demeanor drew the unwavering attention of every girl in the room. Now that she was clean, groomed, fed, and rested, the strange girl glowed with intimidating power. The bear was not moved; it paced, grunted, and snarled.

"That is far from likely, and I expect you know it too well," Psyche replied to what the others heard as guttural animal sounds, as though a conversation was taking place. The bear let a great bellow roll up from its belly. "No, you will not. You will not take one more life. Our battle is between you and me. You will never absorb my power or recreate our race in your image."

Nur-gahl reared up on his hind legs and snarled at the sky before slamming down on the patio and roaring at his prey. Polly had to cover her ears. She sensed the other girls behind her, but she couldn't look away from the bear, its goopy spittle coating the glass.

Psyche sighed as she swept her hand in front of the glass. The door slid open. Polly and the girls cried out, but Psyche stepped forward, unafraid.

The strength of Psyche's telekinetic power held Nur-gahl back. He struggled against the unseen force, his paw restrained above his head as he prepared to strike. Right then, Psyche took a blow from an invisible object. She tumbled backwards with a *snap*. As she slid up to sit and glare at Nur-gahl, Polly noticed her limp shoulder, dislocated at the socket, and slumped backward.

"What do we do?" Polly yelled, nausea roiling in her stomach. Psyche ignored her. Alya bolted to the sliding glass door and slammed it shut. "NO!" screamed Polly as she tried to pull Alya off the lock. "We can't help her, and that thing will kill us all!" Alya grabbed the can of bear spray from Polly's backpack and braced herself to use it.

"Listen to Alya. We need to get out of here." Bethany pulled Polly's arm.

"Our bikes are in the garage. If that thing is distracted, we'll be halfway to town before it knows we're gone." Alya said to Bethany while Brittany struggled to keep Polly back.

"It's all downhill. Should work." Bethany looked at Brittany, who nodded in agreement.

"We have to go before that monster crushes Psyche and moves on to us," said Alya.

Brittany used her free arm to yank a stunned Caroline away from her spot beside the china cabinet. Bethany scooped up their backpacks while the rest ran toward the basement.

The bear roared again as the girls thumped down the stairs. Brittany flung open the door to the Michaels' garage. Polly slapped the switch on the wall and the garage door rumbled up.

"We'll go straight to our house. It's closest. We can call the cops from there." Bethany slung her bag onto her back.

"What if your mom and dad are home?" Caroline asked the twins.

"Then we're all grounded anyway, so who cares!" Alya blurted as she launched out of the garage and down the driveway.

BANG-CRACK—the noise gave way to a tinkling sound from the backyard. Polly knew without seeing: that was the end of her mom's sliding glass door.

"AAAAAHHHHH!" An inhuman cry of attack pierced the air around them.

"Is there any chance she can fight him off?" Polly asked Alya. The latter shook her head. Polly turned for one last look at her house. The wind pushed her hair into her face as they sped along Sagebrush Ridge toward Lakeview Road.

"So how do we convince someone with a gun that a bear with the mind of an alien monster is loose in Bella Vista?" Bethany yelled from the rear of their cycling convoy.

"What would it help if we could? Psyche seemed pretty sure that thing is impossible to kill," Polly said.

"My dad's rifle or shotgun would wound a real bear. Especially the shotgun; it's a twelve gauge." Alya shouted back. "But what's back there is something else."

"We have to hope Psyche can hurt that thing. All we can do for now is warn people." Caroline's voice sounded grave.

"Who should we warn?" asked Brittany.

"Everyone!" Polly shouted.

The final sliver of soft gray light drained from the sky behind them. The streetlights came on as they hit the outskirts of town. Bethany and Brittany's house was dark when the girls rolled up to the front door.

"Our parents must still be at the hospital—it's too late for them to be anywhere else." Bethany unlocked the door and they ran inside, leaving their bikes scattered on the lawn.

"Should we call nine-one-one?" asked Alya.

"I think we should start with animal control. They'll have a better chance of taking down a bear, even a supernatural one," said Brittany.

"If we call the police and tell them it's a bear, they'll turn it over to animal control anyway. If that," Polly said with disdain. "I think we should go straight to the newspaper."

"Whoever we call, I'm sure they'll take us a bit more seriously now that the orchard incident has made the news," Caroline said as the girls filed into the twins' kitchen.

Brittany grabbed the phone book from a drawer in the kitchen island. Bethany grabbed a cordless phone from a cradle on the counter, waiting impatiently for her sister to recite a number.

"I do not want your authorities to get involved," Psyche said, appearing out of nowhere from the shadows down the hall. "Nur-gahl is my responsibility and I will not allow humans to die fighting him."

"What the *hell*!" shouted Brittany.

"Psyche!" Polly blurted, equally shocked and delighted.

"Provided I know where I am going, I can transport myself intra-dimensionally over short distances without physical or mental side effects." Psyche spoke as though stating obvious facts. "I left Nur-gahl neutralized, but he will not remain so for long."

"Neutralized how?" Alya looked unconvinced.

"I impaled him with a large piece of Polly's glass door. He is pinned to the ground, but he will regain his strength and push free in a matter of hours."

"What happens if Polly's mom finds a not-quite-dead demon bear slashed up in her backyard?" Bethany demanded.

"I'm more worried about her freaking when she sees the door destroyed. It probably took half the kitchen with it," said Polly.

"And part of your roof, regrettably," added Psyche.

"So, I say again," Caroline said, taking a deep breath. "We're a bunch of kids. We can't help you kill a demon bear from another dimension."

"All I need you to do is arm me. I require resources that you can help me locate. I thought we had more time to prepare. I am sorry to ask for these things suddenly. Worry not; I will do the wounding and killing."

"What do you need? It can't be more silver. I'm still wondering if I can pull that off . . ."

"To destroy his essence, I need to collapse a fissure in spacetime with

Nur-gahl trapped inside. The moment of closure lasts only part of a second, making the task nearly impossible to accomplish during battle. Or I can leave him formless in a barren wasteland with no life forms or organic matter from which to regenerate; however, my finding a lifeless world is almost impossible as my portals are drawn to life. My energy can penetrate the barriers of the multiverse, but its compass always seeks life and I cannot control the destination. I have searched, at random, for a living world at the moment of its death. To increase my odds of success, I must also weaken Nur-gahl significantly before pulling him into such a world. We fight after every journey. Yet here, I detected a plentiful mineral which may help substantially. A few handfuls of sodium chloride—salt."

"That's it?" shouted Bethany. "I'll tackle this thing myself then." She reached for a salt shaker atop the dining table.

"Couldn't you open a portal and throw him at it? Wouldn't he just dissolve on contact, from what you say?" Polly massaged her face with her hands.

"Once Nur-gahl is formless, I will be momentarily unsure of his where-abouts. He could enter the fissure, but he may be strong enough to slip back out and remain on this plane. During that time, I will deteriorate mentally until my brain reboots entirely, leaving me totally vulnerable. Because he desires to consume my essence, and by extension my abilities, my presence near him on the other side will be the only leverage I can achieve. After a few seconds, a fissure closes on its own, leaving your home safe with Nur-gahl and I secure and as far from you as possible." Psyche's features betrayed no emotion as she seated herself at the kitchen table. "Please keep in mind that unless I open a portal to a planet or dimension I have already experienced—which would be pointless, as I have never been pulled to a barren realm—I cannot be certain what is on the other side. If I force him through a fissure blindly, I could end up throwing him into a pool of innocent victims. Here or there, it will only take a matter of hours for Nur-gahl to absorb organic matter and generate a new form." Psyche folded her hands on the table and waited.

"Okay, so this can't possibly be a simple matter of throwing salt on a raging bear." Alya sized up Brittany, who gripped the salt shaker as though ready for action.

"I should attempt to cause an explosion at Nur-gahl's center of mass while distributing the salt through his flesh. It will require substantial concentration and a weapon capable of putting a hole in a large creature." Psyche looked around expectantly. Polly joined her at the table, slumped down, and sighed.

"I guess we'll need my dad's guns." Alya drew in a long breath.

"Gun, singular. Only one girl here has ever fired a gun before. Unless you think it's the kind of thing you can teach in an afternoon?" Bethany raised an eyebrow.

"I could probably fire a gun. How hard can it be? Point, pull, and BOOM!" Brittany simulated an explosion with her hands.

"Bethany's right. I'm barely able to operate a shotgun safely. It's not a good plan to learn to shoot while running for your life. Especially when your friends can all easily get in the way." Alya massaged her temples.

Psyche tilted her head, peering into Alya's mind. "You will use your father's shotgun loaded with regular metal ball bullets to tear into Nur-gahl. Then you will fire a bullet full of salt. From there, I will use psychic energy to pull him open and destroy his earthly form. Where can we acquire this 'rock salt' that is on all your minds?"

The girls paused in amazement.

"Valley Hardware, downtown." Polly took a deep breath as she visualized Psyche's plan.

"Then let us go now," said Psyche.

"They'll be closed." Bethany looked out the window toward town.

"We have no time to lose." Psyche started toward the door.

"If I'm going to break into one or more jewelers over the next couple of days, we might not want the police any more on guard than they already are. Robbing a hardware store for something we can just buy is a bad move." Polly caught Psyche at the door.

"We could also use some sleep." Brittany rubbed her eyes.

"Mom and Dad are probably going to be gone all night. We can sleep and start off first thing in the morning," said Bethany.

Psyche considered the proposal with a frown. "I will leave at sunrise, alone if necessary."

"We've got your back, don't worry." Polly led Psyche into the living room.

And as soon as she laid back on the plush loveseat across the room, Polly felt sleep crash over her like muggy fog.

Chapter 15

Rumbling traffic nudged Polly awake as dim early morning light spilled into the twins' living room. Her orchard-adjacent home was serenaded by valley winds and the occasional coyote, so waking up to more typically city sounds felt strange.

Polly looked at the wall opposite where she lay. A portrait of the twins posing in their matching spandex jazz dance outfits, complete with pink slouch socks and sandy blonde perms, struck a sharp contrast to the two disheveled girls out cold on the couch below—Alya and Caroline's heads at opposite ends, their bodies buried under a single giant quilt. She assumed the twins were asleep in their own beds. But where was Psyche? *Dr. and Mrs. Johnsons' bed? I hope not!*

Cold air rushed over Polly as she pushed away the floral comforter and got up. She rubbed her arms as she wandered from the living room to the kitchen. She caught sight of Psyche's long platinum hair standing just outside, on the Johnsons' lush, manicured lawn wearing only Polly's old plaid shirt and gazing up at an overcast sky. The sunroom next to the kitchen was the warmest part of the twins' house, but Polly still shuddered watching Psyche's bare, porcelain legs in the morning breeze. Polly made no sound, but Psyche turned and looked directly at her benefactor. She seemed to float as she strode gracefully across the cold, dewy grass.

"Do not worry, I cannot feel the cold here as much as when I first arrived," said Psyche as she entered the sunroom and shut the glass door behind her. "My body has recovered, but my mind is still adjusting. This region is so polluted with telepathic noise; I wanted to feel bare ground beneath my feet and concentrate on my breathing. But that is done. We must rouse the others. We need to obtain our supplies. Nur-gahl has woken, too. I can hear his thoughts."

"Let's start by getting your pants back on," said Polly, listening as footfalls slapped the tile floor beside her.

"Whoa, were you just outside barefoot?" Brittany stretched her arms up and clasped her hands together.

"Bare-legged, too, from the looks of it," added Bethany.

"I will find the rest of my garments right away. We must be off to find salt quickly. Nur-gahl is awake and nursing his wounds. The longer we wait, the stronger he will become." Psyche retreated down the hall to the twins' guest room, which Polly had forgotten existed.

"And hanging around increases the chances of our parents coming home, which will end in a long list of chores. Coffee first though." Brittany yawned and went over to the kitchen counter, and dumped two scoops of grounds into a coffee maker.

"I have a bad feeling about this whole plan," Caroline said, appearing at the entrance to the kitchen with Alya at her side.

"Speaking of bad feelings, at what point, Polly, are you planning to rob a jewelry store?" Alya asked as she rubbed her eyes.

"Do you even know which one you'll . . . hit?" asked Caroline. She arched her eyebrows sympathetically.

"Our friend the cat burglar." Brittany smirked as she arranged some mugs, sugar, and spoons on the kitchen counter.

"I think it can wait until after we've taken out this bear. Mom has that long at least, I'm pretty sure." Polly brushed her hair while staring thoughtfully through the sunroom windows.

Bethany took two boxes out of their freezer and held them up, offering a choice between blueberry waffles and strawberry strudel.

"Waffles for me, please," said Caroline.

"I'll take some strudel," said Alya.

"I really, really, didn't want to do this, but . . ." Caroline sat next to Polly at the table. "I think I can help get you into a jeweler, when the time comes."

Bethany and Brittany served up six coffees, glancing scandalously at one another as Polly leaned into Caroline's face. "Spill it!" Polly said.

"My uncle works at Sun Valley Jewelers, the one on Main and Tenth. He won't help us, but I might be able to get you his keys. I don't know if they've got a big pile of silver. Maybe right after they receive a new shipment." Caroline took a deep regret-filled breath.

"Thank you!" Polly sprang a hug on Caroline that knocked the wind out of her.

"Don't thank me yet. I'm going to jail with you if we get caught. And my parents will hate me."

"Caroline, you'd be saving a life," said Bethany. Brittany nodded her approval through a bite of pastry.

"Let's not get ahead of ourselves. We've got something bigger and scarier to worry about first." Caroline gulped her coffee, accepting her waffle with a grateful nod.

"Very true. We must leave. Now." Psyche reappeared wearing Polly's pants, poised to break into a run.

"We should start at Valley Hardware just off the highway. We all know where it is." Bethany transferred their coffee mugs to the sink. Alya and Caroline left to wash their faces.

Minutes later, a row of six girls on five bikes sped along the shoulder of the highway. Brittany and Bethany rode their own twelve-speeds alongside Alya, Caroline, and Polly's beat-up old mountain bikes. Psyche rode as Polly's passenger, clinging awkwardly to the latter's back as she pedaled hard toward their destination.

They didn't bother with locks, practically throwing their bikes into the racks in front of the hardware store. The red plastic sign with its large white maple leaf and fluorescent interior gave off a dull glow under the silver sky.

"Hey, guys, do you think Nick Hauser's working today?"

Brittany's playful tone shot a rock through Polly's gut. "Does it matter?" she said as heat filled her face at the thought of Nick and his dashing leather jacket.

"Focus, ladies," said Alya as she led the procession through the automatic doors.

Inside, Bethany cornered the first employee she could find. "Excuse me," she said, "could you tell us where to find rock salt?"

A rotund woman with orange peel skin frowned at them. "What do you girls want with rock salt? It's almost summer, you know."

"It's for our dad. He's got a cabin in the mountains and they still get snow up there." Bethany seemed so comfortable with telling spontaneous lies. Polly envied her.

"Well, we've packed most of it into storage until October. You might find a bag or two at the back. Go ask at the Garden Center." The woman turned and headed in the direction of lighting and paint. Her red golf shirt clung to folds of her back, her shoulders slumped.

"I wonder if she'd be more helpful if one of our parents had asked," said Caroline, glaring at the woman as she walked away.

"Let's find the Garden Center and get on with this," said Alya. Her grouchy mood had Polly wondering what she was angry about—the bear hunt or the potential jewelry heist. Likely both, she decided, following her friend while the rest of them trailed right behind.

"Well, it looks like he is here," Alya said. She'd noticed Nick a heartbeat before Polly. He was making notes on a clipboard at a cash register positioned between two isles of potted tree seedlings.

Bethany slid on over to him. "Hey, there, Nick." She smiled.

Polly felt like throwing up as she noticed how warmly Nick smiled back at Bethany. And then she caught sight of Psyche in her peripheral vision and saw the look on Nick's face as he sized-up the new girl.

"Hey, Bethany. And girls. What can I do for you?" A generous layer of dust coated his upper body, some of it in among his dark brown curls. He brushed some of the dust from his hair and set his clipboard aside. His relaxed, bright expression disarmed Polly.

"We need rock salt. Do you still have it or not?" Alya's flat, disgruntled tone made Polly want to apologize, but her mouth was too dry to get a word out.

"What do you need rock salt for?" Nick looked from Alya to Bethany and Brittany. His forest green eyes rested on Polly for only a moment before he went back to gawking at Psyche.

"She's new in town. We'll tell you all about it at school," said Bethany, doing her best to sound both polite and urgent. "We're kind of in a rush, though. My dad is going up to our cabin, and he's worried there'll still be ice and snow. I told him we'd hurry back as soon as possible."

"Are you all going?" Nick regarded Polly again as he came out from behind the kiosk. He stood in front of her, taller than she remembered and smelling of something woodsy. Polly froze, managing only a smile.

"Yes. And their dad hates waiting." Alya answered quickly, looking from Nick to the twins. Caroline and Psyche stayed equally quiet, hovering behind Polly.

"I'm sure I can hook you up. Meet me at the front. I'll bring it up for you."

The six of them headed back to the front of the store. Polly blocked out the rest of her friends' conversation as they waited for Nick at the customer service desk. He appeared a moment later carrying a giant bag on his shoulder like she would a beach towel. With his large hands he gripped the canvas cover and hefted the bag onto the counter.

"Anything else I can help you with? Should I pack this out to your dad's car?" Nick smiled at Bethany. A dagger of rage darted out from Polly's heart.

"Nope. We're good." Brittany handed a ten-dollar bill to the cashier. Nick nodded and turned to leave.

Alya and Bethany each took an end of the canvas bag while Polly ran ahead to hold the door for them.

Outside in the parking lot, Bethany produced some bungee cords and meticulously strapped the bag of salt to the back of Alya's mountain bike, as it was the only one equipped with a rack.

Back on the road, Bethany waited until they were out of the Valley Hardware parking lot before shouting at Polly: "I bet if you start listening to the Cure, you'll find more of an excuse to talk to Nick at school."

"Never mind talking about music; she's going to have to manage at least a word first." Brittany's sly smile blossomed into a cheeky grin.

"Even if I cared what Nick likes—which I don't—I'm sure he isn't the least bit interested in my taste, either. And I've talked to him before." Polly hated having to yell anything on the subject of Nick Hauser as they pedaled along a very public road.

"Leave her alone, Brittany." A hint of pity laced Bethany's words. Polly's chest felt hollow.

"Hey, Psyche, what was that dark-haired boy thinking back in the store?"

"Don't answer that, Psyche," Alya fired off before Psyche's pale lips could even part.

Please, if you can hear me, let this conversation die. Polly aimed her thought at the space directly behind her.

"If you wish," Psyche said just loud enough for Polly to hear.

They stopped at Alya's house long enough for her to sneak into the tool shed in the back yard. It was secured with a padlock, but she had a key for it on her keychain. It was only a few minutes before she reappeared with a long, padded case slung over her shoulder, and then they took off again.

Minutes later, they skidded to a halt on the twins' driveway, narrowly missing the black Cadillac parked there—Bethany and Brittany's parents were home.

Chapter 16

"Looks like we might get a couple of parents involved after all," said Alya, resting her bike against the garage door. She handed her case off to Caroline and unwrapped the beefy bag of salt before propping it next to the gun, against the exterior of the house.

"Mom and Dad are probably already sleeping off their night shifts." Brittany eyed the living room window for signs of movement.

"Yeah, they won't be too worried about what we're doing unless we're loud," Bethany confirmed as she fished her keys out of her pocket and opened the front door.

"Good morning, girls!" The twins' mom beamed a pleasant, yet weary, smile at them from the hallway. Mrs. Johnson was carrying a full laundry basket, still in her mint-green scrubs.

"What sent you all out so early on a Sunday morning?" their dad asked, sounding surprisingly chipper as he appeared at the entrance to the kitchen. He wore a collared shirt and gray slacks which looked, like his salt-and-pepper hair, as though they had been rumpled from a long night.

Panic throbbed inside Polly as she frantically tried to problem solve. Were the Johnson's getting ready to go to bed? If not, where and how would the girls implement their shotgun shell conversion plan. Back at her house? Would her mom be home? Would the bear be mobile, angry, and prowling around the property?

"Oh, just out for a bike ride. Staying active and all that good stuff." Bethany added a little wiggle and a disco move.

"It's barely warm enough. I think we'll wait another couple of weeks for the morning next ride." Brittany's tone with her parents was utterly angelic compared to how she spoke with her friends.

Polly regarded the twins' parents, taking a moment to relish her ability to be herself around her mom. Psyche smiled at her. *Get out of my head,* Polly thought but smiled back. Polly's mental image of her mother quickly updated to the version of her that had dark circles under the eyes and waxy, thin skin. Soon her mom would be wearing a head scarf to hide the fact that her hair is falling out. *This is why I need your help.* Polly looked away from Psyche and concentrated on an abstract painting on the living room wall, to try and shove the sadness down—to keep her tears at bay.

"So, what do you girls have planned this afternoon?" The twins' dad was one of those adults who tried to sound like he was talking to a peer when he spoke to kids. In Polly's mind, he never managed to be convincing, always retaining a hint of that too-loud, too-happy demeanor of people uncomfortable being around children.

"Ummmm . . ." Bethany chewed on her finger, stalling. Polly's eyes widened. If Bethany couldn't think of a lie, they were screwed.

"Uh, well . . ." Brittany couldn't come up with anything either. The confused look on their mother's face deepened.

The phone rang and Polly lurched. Their mother rushed to the coffee table and scooped the receiver into her hand.

"Hello? . . . No, Jim, we've only been home for . . . Okay. We're on our way."

"He didn't seriously ask you to go back, did he?" Brittany's eyes were full of sympathy. Bethany shot her sister a dark side-eye.

"It can't be helped, girls. Don, there's been some kind of hunting accident north of the lake. Can I talk to you in the hall?"

Polly was desperate to follow them and hear what exactly had happened at the lake. Bethany took a step forward and her dad shouted her name. The

Johnsons retreated to their bedroom and shut the door.

"Psyche, can you tell us what they're saying?" asked Brittany.

"Can you? We need to know if it's Nur-gahl, and how bad the attack was." Polly felt certain their sleepy little town had not just seen a random "accident" such as this.

Psyche nodded. Her gaze drifted off in the direction the Johnsons had gone.

Moments passed agonizingly but the girls remained silent. "The man who called them," Psyche said, "named Jim, he used the word 'mauling' when describing the accident victims. One is dead already, five more are receiving intensive medical care." Psyche looked at Bethany and then Brittany. "Your parents will be needed at the hospital for several hours. Your father will be performing surgery this afternoon."

Footsteps broke the girls' concentration. Dr. Johnson reappeared, followed by his wife. He sighed and collected his wallet and keys off the counter. "Your mother is right. It can't be helped. We'll be back as soon as we can. Don't go out looking for trouble," he added with a wink.

Psyche balled her fists. Polly moved in front of her and aimed her thoughts back. *It's just a figure of speech; something people say for no reason. He doesn't know anything about Nur-gahl.*

Minutes later the black Cadillac was backing out of the driveway. Bethany peeked through the living room blinds to make sure they weren't coming back.

"That took care of itself," said Alya, brushing her hands together.

"How can you say such a thing?" Psyche looked at Alya, horrified. "Those men—it was Nur-gahl, without a doubt. He has killed already and will kill again! I should have stayed to banish him. My neglect, my failure caused those deaths." Her silky pearl hair swung around as she turned to gauge Polly's reaction. "We can waste no more time! WE MUST LEAVE NOW!" Psyche grew inconsolable as she paced around the room.

"Psyche, we have nothing to fight with except your bare hands. If he's strong enough to attack already, we have no choice but to stick to our plan," said Bethany. She reached out to Psyche, to try and comfort her, but thought twice and withdrew.

Psyche glared around the room before storming out the front door.

"Wait, Psyche!" Polly ran after her.

Psyche whirled around and Polly collided suddenly with an invisible wall. There was no pain, but she couldn't move. Her lips refused to close. Her voice failed her.

Psyche's glare deepened to a furious glower. Polly felt warmth prickling all over. She tried calling out again.

Please, Psyche, you're going to hurt me. I want to help you. We all do.

"I should never have dealt with mortals. This is my responsibility. Alone." Psyche's words chilled Polly. Still frozen, riddled with panic, Polly watched as Psyche turned her head and a bright light enveloped the pale girl's silhouette. The light subsided and Psyche was gone.

"NO!" Polly fell to her knees. "YOU CAN'T GO!" She started to sob. "You're her only chance." Phrases like "malignant mass" and "forty to fifty percent survival rate" invaded Polly's head for the first time since spying a balloon of electricity over the orchard behind her house.

"Polly?" Alya appeared next to her on the lawn.

"She left. She was going to cure Mom and now she left!" Polly sobbed, but she felt rage swirling to life around her core.

"Maybe she's just going to fight Nur-gahl alone. She could still keep her promise. I don't think she's the sort of person who would bail."

"She's not a person at all! Who knows what she'll do. Goddammit!" Polly kicked the concrete step under the Johnsons' front door and hopped on her good foot to recover. She looked up to contain her tears.

"We know where she's gone. Come inside and help us convert the shells. We'll be back at your mom's place soon."

Polly nodded and followed Alya into the spotless Tudor façade.

"I'll start emptying shells," said Alya.

"I'll help you. Just show me what to do," said Caroline.

"Let's grab the salt," Bethany said to Brittany.

Polly cleared papers from the dining table. Alya and Caroline got to work quickly while Polly transferred empty shell casings to the counter where the twins refilled them with rock salt. After Alya had finished emptying the casings, she took a spot beside the twins to help reassemble the shells. Only Alya knew how to do it properly—none of the girls argued.

"I think that's it." Alya stepped back and put her hands on her hips.

Caroline brushed the loose crumbs off the counter and Polly stowed the resealed bag of salt next to the fridge.

The process had taken less than an hour. And after repacking their bags, all five girls pedaled with all their might back to the Michaels' house next to Lakeview Hills orchard. Polly's mom's small sky-blue Honda hatchback sat in the driveway. The girls threw their bikes on the lawn and ran around back. And then:

"Polly Elaine Michaels, WHAT IN THE SAM HILL HAVE YOU DONE TO MY HOUSE!"

Polly froze again, and this time she had no idea how to answer.

Chapter 17

"WHAT IS THIS? What happened here?" screamed Mom. She paced back and forth across the patio, broken glass crunching with each step.

"Mom, it's not our fault! There was a bear!" Polly closed the distance to her mom, but stopped short, sensing the pure rage emanating from her. "Look at the blood! We're not lying!"

"A bear? How—" Mom caught sight of the blood and her breathing grew rapid.

"Ms. Michaels, everything is under control. Psyche had this . . . well no *we* . . . called Animal Control and . . ." Bethany's inspiration dried up. She shot a panicked look at her sister.

"We brought a gun, so we're prepared if it comes back," said Brittany.

"You . . . WHAT?" Mom gasped and her body went slack. She fell backwards and landed on the grass with a *whump*.

"She must be in shock," said Bethany.

"Polly call nine-one-one," said Brittany.

"Mom!" Polly ignored Brittany and rushed to her mom's side. Alya tiptoed carefully through the glass minefield and whisked the phone off the wall.

"Wake up, Mom." Polly turned to Bethany. "Grab her legs. Let's get her up to bed."

"Polly, we should wait for the paramedics." Bethany checked Polly's mom's pulse while Brittany listened for her breathing.

"They're on their way," Alya said, rejoining the group.

"What can we do for her while we wait?" Caroline kneeled down next to Polly.

"All we can do is keep her safe," said Bethany. She rubbed her arms against the breeze. Brittany looked to her sister for a hint at what to do next. The calmer sister shook her head.

"Do we still want to go chasing after Psyche?" Alya stepped back and looked around the corner to the driveway and Sagebrush Ridge, attempting to will an ambulance to appear.

"We have to! She's Mom's only hope. Once she calms down about those hunters, I have to believe she'll remember her promise. She's not human, but she has a heart." Polly sobbed as she held her mom's hand and brushed hair from her forehead. Her mom let out a murmur. Polly prayed the collapse was shock and not the cancer. Either way, it looked like death had its finger on her mom's heart.

Finally, an ambulance arrived and two men in navy blue bombers with medical emblems on their sleeves hurried over. Alya led Polly into the house, leaving the twins to answer the paramedics' questions while Caroline and Alya made Polly a cup of tea.

"I know this is hard," Caroline said, "but you should go to the hospital with your mom."

"Why? What can I do for her there? Half the hospital already knows she has cancer. The paramedics and doctors can help her, not me. The only thing I can do is get Psyche back. God, what if that thing's killed her already?" Polly set her tea aside and put her head in her hands. "No. I don't have time to cry." She marched back out to the paramedics with her game face on.

"Miss, we need to take your mother to the hospital," said one paramedic while the other used straps to secure Polly's mom to a stretcher. Her mom was awake, barely. Polly rushed to her side.

"I'm going to stay here and wait for the police," Polly said to her mom. "We called about the house. I'll catch up to you at the hospital after. Then I'll stay at Bethany and Brittany's." She was lying better than Bethany now. Polly suppressed a smile, pleased with herself, but still aware of her audience.

"Sweetie, I'm so sorry I yelled. I'm sorry I'm sick. I'm glad you're okay. I don't know what I'd do . . ." Her mom broke off, closing her eyes as the energy drained out of her.

"Don't worry, Mom, I'm fine." Polly squeezed her mom's hand.

"Are you able to get to the hospital on your own?" one of the paramedics asked, looking around the backyard as if to suggest that the girls could be in danger if left alone.

"We've got bikes," said Alya.

"And we can call our parents," said Caroline.

"Don't wait too long before you come. Once your mother's been processed through the ER, she could be admitted overnight, and visiting hours end at four." The paramedics lifted the stretcher in unison and carried Polly's mom to the ambulance. Its piercing siren wailed, fading as the flashing red and white lights sped away, back to downtown Bella Vista.

"Okay, we've got work to do," Polly said to the group. She shoved the heels of her hands into her eyes and rubbed away her tears.

"Alya, can you pick up Psyche's trail from here?" Polly stood next to the kitchen table and peered out the glass door, into the orchard beyond.

"Even in all that mess?" Brittany's doubt earned a glare from Bethany.

"Of course she can." Caroline stood tall.

"Let's find out." Alya jogged back out to where Nur-gahl had been pinned by a huge piece of glass. "I see a couple of bloody paw prints here. They lead back into the orchard. I don't see anything from Psyche, but if she came back here, she probably followed this trail, too."

Alya hefted the shotgun onto her back and marched into the trees, holding the gun's strap as she walked. Polly followed directly behind, carrying her backpack stuffed with ammo. Brittany, Bethany, and Caroline brought up the rear.

The girls allowed Alya to monitor the bear tracks in silence. As the blood grew sparse and the trail became overgrown with orchard debris, she concentrated, paused, assessed, continued, and repeated, again and again.

Polly's heart was ready to explode by the time they crested a hill deep in the orchard and heard voices. Men's voices.

They were arguing.

Chapter 18

Psyche closed the portal behind her and dropped to her knees on the lawn near the glass and wood chaos of Polly's patio. She had not been totally honest with the human girls about the ease of intra-dimensional travel. Her head swam for a moment. She recovered, and then looked to the large, jagged piece of bloody glass that no longer restrained Nur-gahl. *This will not do. Polly's mom will be terrified.* Psyche telekinetically launched the red glass off into a pile of leaves at the back of the property.

Frustration drove her to examine the rest of scene for too long. A puddle of blood remained. Psyche stared at the wreckage, willing the bear to return to the scene. *That new attack was on the other side of this orchard. He will not have gone far afterwards. He has fed, so he will be resting yet recharged, his thoughts loud.*

Psyche closed her eyes and extended her mind out into the orchard, sweeping through the trees for her adversary. In her mind's eye she saw a dim dream-like version of the orchard under a dark and overcast sky. Her view glided smoothly through the trees, up over a hill, and then another, until a wave of blood rose up and engulfed her. Human memories from the victims rushed into Psyche's brain in an explosion of pictures and chatter. She could make no sense of the data, excepting the final surge of adrenaline at the end as she made out the image of a demon bear's enormous, snarling jaws, followed by searing pain as a giant paw, claws splayed, filled her view. Psyche opened her eyes and pulled out of the vision, gulping on nothing as she centered herself in her physical location. She retained the image of a mountain of bloody fur feasting on a limp body, just past the far western border of the orchard.

I have no time. I must create another fissure.

Psyche reached out and electric sparks crackled across her fingertips. She carved a bright blue oval shape in the air and waited until it was large enough to enter.

Weakened again, Psyche kneeled to recover. She instantly saw the giant bear fewer than ten feet away, snoring through a glutinous dream. She rammed her hand in her pants pocket and found the heavy cache of pennies she had stolen from the twins' kitchen. She emptied the contents of her fist into her mouth and braced herself, perched on all four limbs while her body absorbed the metal. Psyche felt hot vibrations shooting from her core through her veins and into her muscles. She clenched her teeth to hold back the pressure building in her chest as she watched the slumbering bear's heap of fur rise and fall with each deep breath. She let out a sudden belch of electricity.

Psyche mentally uprooted a broken dead tree and swung it like a bat at the healing wound on the bear's abdomen. The beast snorted as the trunk knocked its body along the ground. Odors of raw earth and fresh blood wafted at her.

"Wake up, Nur-gahl. Your time here is done."

"Uggggggh," he grunted.

The bear sleepily rolled over and red ooze spilled from a barely closed wound in his belly. Nur-gahl struggled to rise, concentrated, and shook his muzzle, spraying red around his head. "Child, you underestimate my strength. I have fed and I am healing. I can draw minerals directly from the surface of this world. None of your antiquated party tricks will work. If you had spent more of your youth honing your mind and less time playing at Temple politics, you would be incredibly strong. But you are not."

The bear swiped at the air pitifully, but his telekinetic energy was still enough to knock Psyche to the ground. She landed with a thud, wincing as the impact expelled the air from her lungs.

You will never take me. She directed the thought at Nur-gahl's beady black eyes and launched to her feet. She ran east into the orchard.

Psyche stared at the leaf-covered horizon that appeared between two rows of trees. She ran hard, using psychic energy to propel her body with each footfall, giving her a gravity defying stride, faster than she could otherwise run. She listened for the heavy sounds of a bear behind her while frantically reaching ahead with her mind, praying not to be distracted by human thoughts.

She forced out images of guns and salt and the girls' faces, knowing Nur-gahl would be probing her mind as she in turn searched for a safe and isolated place. Satisfied by the crude clearing made by their first battle, Psyche came to a halt. She turned and braced herself for the attack.

Seconds later, Nur-gahl blasted through the tree line. He barreled toward Psyche *RAAAAAWWR*-ing at the top of his lungs. She held her ground, using every scrap of focus she had to erect a telekinetic shield around her body.

Nur-gahl didn't break stride as he swiped a dagger-tipped baseball mitt paw at Psyche's face. The strength of his own telekinetic power and the physical force behind his claws broke Psyche's shield, rattling her body before his furry trunk of an arm collided with her head.

Four deep red slashes unzipped her porcelain face. A heartbeat later, dark syrup poured out. She screamed and fell backward as her face oozed and throbbed. On all fours now, she lifted her head against the blinding pain and let out a primal scream. Light burst from her mouth and out through her eyes. Using sheer mental will she forced open a new fissure in spacetime. A rippling puddle of phosphorescence hovered beside the mountain of brown fur. Electricity prickled at the edges of the portal, traveling inward—explosions sounded across an unseen new world.

A gunshot blasted beside her. Nur-gahl turned to find the source of the sound. Psyche used the distraction and telekinetically knocked the bear into the fissure. He tumbled on his side halfway into the opening. Flames licked the bear's fur, the acrid stink of it carrying on the wind. Psyche leapt up, finishing the job by physically shoving the bear's rear into the portal. She tumbled in after him and the light flicked off.

The scraped-up patch of earth beneath them and a rumpled pile of Polly's old clothes was all that remained.

Sy'kai awoke inside a violent dust storm on ground that felt somehow rocky and gelatinous. She could see little more than a few feet ahead of her in every direction.

She tried to force herself to stand, and went to shield her eyes from the dust as she turned in a circle. No sign of life greeted her, and she soon became aware that she didn't need to shield her eyes because she didn't have any. She didn't need to stand, either, as she had no legs—and no body.

With no body to heal, Sy'kai's mind recovered quickly. She had spent so long in physical form, becoming one creature, then another, and another. Like thousands of other morphlings, she had long taken alien forms to inhabit worlds and learn, always to populate volumes of knowledge in the vast libraries of the Astral Temple. But after the Great War, her transformations became part of hunting the evil Nur-gahl, for both justice and atonement. *Could this finally be a newly barren plane? Have I succeeded?* Sy'kai giggled like a child at the prospect of finally being so close to thwarting her nemesis. *I KNEW IT! FINALLY! WE ARE HERE!*

Sy'kai struggled to breathe, only to realize again that she had no need. She felt more of her memory returning. To move without a body, she simply needed to think of where she wanted to be, limited only by her vision in this unexplored dimension. *Oh, how I have missed the simple bliss of being nothing but a consciousness.*

What have you done, you petulant brat? Are you really so righteous as to maroon us both at the edge of the universe? What does this achieve?

Anxiety fluttered around Sy'kai and diffused into her. She must now either crush Nur-gahl or evade him forever.

Lost your mind again, have you? It seems that you may have finally found a world at the moment of its death. There are no life forms left to mimic here. Yet. You have isolated us before, but never so far from life as to achieve your goal. Will you return to the Temple if you escape me here? I know I will if I consume you. Such an important gift, yours. The ability to travel from one point in the universe to another, limited only by firsthand knowledge or the presence of life. You and the other precious knowledge-seekers. So righteous and so weak. Sister, if you could only taste the exquisite flavors of terror and anguish. You would be by my side for eternity, devouring every possible scrap of life.

A moment of temptation lingered in Sy'kai. The desire to experience what Nur-gahl described wove into her core and tried to grapple with her true nature. She fought the feeling, drawing on love and compassion to break that dark tendril's grip on her formless heart. Instinct told her to run. Practicality reminded her that she still had no body to run with. Sy'kai focused on the farthest point she could discern on the barren planet's horizon. She surged through the storm, away from the malicious energy behind her. She focused on escape, but the sense of something forgotten nagged at her, crumbling her celebratory mood. One thought popped into Sy'kai's mind: *Save her.*

Sy'kai pushed her consciousness into the space ahead and a portal opened. She raced through and into sweet oxygen-rich air. A second later she was at the core of a violent reaction. Matter and energy swirled around her. She tumbled to the ground, back in a familiar pale, naked body. She stood up, tripped on a pile of clothes, and quickly scooped them up.

"Up here! I think we hit something. I heard it growling!" A man's voice shouted to unseen companions. Sy'kai bolted toward the hill above, past rows of trees, running as hard as her bare feet could carry her.

Chapter 19

Polly ran toward the cluster of police officers, and the hunters wearing vests and khaki uniforms. She knew they'd tell her to get lost, but she had every right to try and find her friend—who also happened to be her mom's best chance at living. If these men couldn't understand that, she'd make them.

"Hello? Excuse me, can you help us?" Polly tilted her head slightly, trying to imitate Bethany's charisma.

"Are you lost, little girl?" An officer in a parks uniform turned away from the group of men. He crossed the scarred ground between them. Up close, he looked too young to be calling Polly a little girl, but she let it slide. Her friends caught up to her. The officer's concerned expression deepened into a frown.

"No, I live on the other side of the orchard. I was out walking with my friends and—" a swell of panic slapped her. Was Alya still carrying a gun? Polly herself had ammunition. She turned to check and let out a puff of breath when she saw Alya's arms empty. She turned to the officer again.

"We heard gun shots," Alya interjected, "so naturally we were concerned. It's not exactly fireworks season. My dad's a hunter and I've been a Girl Guide for ten years, so I know the sound of a gun and"—Alya gestured wildly at the scuffed-up ground—"signs of an animal attack when I see it. Plus, my friend's house was attacked by a huge animal the other night." She pointed to Polly. "We have a right to know what's happening."

Polly felt admiration flowing toward her friend.

"Was anyone hurt?" Bethany said softly. The officer's face and shoulders relaxed.

"No, honey, it was just a snarly old bear. Great big fella, too." The parks officer adjusted his hat. "It's dead now."

"How can you be sure?" Brittany cocked her head.

The officer frowned. "We're sure. You girls should go on back home."

Polly looked from the officer's face back to Alya, then to the twins, and then, standing silent behind them, an increasingly curious Caroline.

"If it's all the same to you, we'd feel better if you let us see for ourselves. My friend's mother was really worried," Caroline said. She was pretty convincing herself, Polly thought.

"Her mother is also a patient of my father's—he's chief physician at Bella Vista General. If we can go back and tell our family friend that she's got nothing to worry about, she'll be able to get some much-needed rest." Bethany's tone had changed from docile to annoyed. She glared at the officer.

"Kenny, what's going on over there?" called a policeman with smoke-gray hair and a bushy mustache.

"Nothing, Pete, just some neighbor kids," Kenny called back.

"This is no place for kids. Move it along now," Pete said, addressing the girls directly.

"We want to know for sure that the bear is dead," Alya demanded, holding her stance.

Polly ignored the implied barrier of authority and walked over to the ring of men still quibbling about how to move the bear's corpse.

"We could let it go one night, maybe two. Like Mark says, it's other animals getting at it that we have to worry about," said the other police officer.

"And if it were rabid, anything that feeds on it could get sick. We need a pack of rabid coyotes like we need holes in our heads." A man with a shaggy blond beard wearing a puffy green vest and a trucker cap glared at Polly as she approached. Alya marched up right behind her.

"What size round did you use? How many kill shots did you land?" Alya's fearlessness did not impress the officers and hunters.

"Listen, kid, if you don't know a dead bear when you see one, I don't know what we can do for you." Officer Pete adjusted his belt and stuck out his chest in Alya's direction.

"Answer the questions. Or is that information confidential?" Polly crossed her arms.

Pete sighed. "I'm about done with this conversation. I'll tell you what we *will* do. My colleague here, Officer Ward, will write you all citations for trespassing. I have a standing request from the owners of Lakeview Hills to detain or escort off the property all unauthorized visitors."

"It was a powerful bear, right? What's wrong with being really sure it's dead?" Bethany did her best to sound respectful.

"Why don't you visit the body later, at the vet's cold storage in town." Pete's tone was sarcastic, laced with anger. "For now, get the hell outta Dodge." He turned his back on the girls, ending their conversation.

"Yes sir, Officer. We hear you loud and clear." Polly did a one hundred and eighty-degree turn and marched back into the orchard. She bent low and scooped something white off the ground as she walked past.

"Polly!" Alya and Brittany called in unison, equally exasperated.

Polly jogged into the trees until she felt sure she was out of earshot of the men. She waited for her friends to catch up, turning a small piece of fabric over in her hands.

"She was here!" Polly whispered as the others caught up to her. She thrust a lace scrunchie out as evidence.

"Psyche?" said Brittany at regular volume. Everyone frowned at her. "Oh, come on, they can't hear and don't care."

"Polly, are you sure?" Alya's hard face softened.

"That *is* the same one I gave her," said Bethany.

"Psyche said that when she passes through a door to another world, her body is destroyed and any possessions are left behind." Polly glanced from one girl to the next.

"Then the scrunchie proves she left this world anyway? Even though she killed Nur-gahl?" Caroline spoke slowly, rubbing her chin.

Polly looked to the late afternoon sun, which had just dropped behind the treetops. "If she passed through her portal-thing, we should have found everything she had on her. My clothes. A couple of jelly bracelets I gave her. And that scrunchie. So, where's the rest of it? Maybe she lost the hair tie in the fight and ran off to heal. We know she doesn't like the idea of going to a hospital."

"If she went toe to toe with a supernatural bear and won, why would she run away?" Alya spoke slowly and calmly.

Polly furrowed her brow. "We can ask her when we find her. Are you willing to try and track her?"

"Even if I were, how far will we get with the redneck patrol at our backs?"

"We'll go back to my place and wait them out," said Polly.

"By the time they clear out, we'll have lost the light." Alya eyed the horizon. "But I'll spend the night at your place again if you want."

"We'll stay, too." Brittany looked at Bethany, who nodded.

"Me too. I need to call my parents again, but I'm sure they'll let me stay," said Caroline. "And Polly, even if we can't find Psyche, your mom can still get better." She touched Polly's forearm.

"My dad says she's getting the best care on the West Coast. The program she's in has the latest drugs." Bethany touched Polly's other arm.

"And there's no way to be sure that even if I stole a crapload of silver and risked going to jail, Psyche would actually turn up and be able to perform some kind of magic cure." Polly started off in the direction of her house. "I still believe she can do it. After I saw her abilities, what she could do . . . after she said she could at least try . . . I felt like Mom had already been saved."

Polly plodded along in silence, her friends staying a few paces behind. As they walked, they heard only the sound of their feet squashing the damp earth.

A clatter of wood planks cracked in the distance and the girls jumped. Polly looked at her friends, and then back in the direction of her house.

"It must have been pieces of the wall or roof falling," said Polly. They jogged back to the old farmhouse and found it half ruined as before.

"We should go back to our place for the night," said Bethany. "Sorry, Polly, but it's safer. For all we know, your roof could cave in at any moment."

"What if . . ." Polly didn't have the heart to say the rest out loud.

"If Psyche's alive, she can take care of herself," said Brittany.

"At least the orchard and hills are safe now." Alya looked toward the top of the far-off hills. A coyote howled in the night.

"Safe if you're a shape-shifting alien warrior," said Bethany.

"Come on, guys, it's getting cold again." Caroline picked up her bike.

Polly cast one more concerned glance back at the darkening hills before mounting her own bike and leading the way back down her driveway. The coyote howled again. The pack of girls ignored its plea and sped toward town.

Chapter 20

Sy'kai walked aimlessly along the border of trees, wracking her brain for a sign of what to do next. She looked back at the setting sun at the exact right moment to knock over a pile of wood planks propped against a cherry tree. She had been following the trail next to the orchard, hoping the cultivated trees would lead to a more significant sign of civilization. The world around her seemed recognizable, but huge gaps of her identity were missing. She had something to do, but she couldn't remember what it was. A voice in her head was certain of one fact: her name was Sy'kai.

She rubbed her arms as she stomped through decaying wild weeds. The grassland next to the trees provided the reassurance of cover, although Sy'kai couldn't pinpoint what exactly made her so anxious. A creature took flight from the inside of a tree and she flinched. An animal howled and she jumped. Her heart raced and she flung her body against a tree in a desperate bid for protection. The gentle wind rustling through the leaves chilled her enough to finally motivate her to move.

I am not in danger. I merely need shelter and a chance to rest. Why am I so afraid? This land feels familiar.

Sy'kai caught sight of a wood structure in the trees. A memory sparked in her brain—she ran to the shed, scanning the orchard in every direction like a fugitive. Once inside the small building, she barred the door with a heavy box. She searched her body for signs of the device she needed. There was nothing. Dejected, she sat in the corner of the room and put her head in her hands.

Wait, what? Is it that easy?

She made fists and felt the presence of a foreign object in her right hand. Intuition compelled her and she pinched the internal orb with her left thumb and forefinger. A blinding flash of a thousand images seared her eyes and she lost consciousness.

After spending another night at Bethany and Brittany's house, Polly had no choice but to go to school Monday morning. The only reason Polly hadn't been sent home like Alya and Caroline was that the twins' parents knew firsthand that Polly's mom had been admitted to the hospital. And after learning about the damage done to her home, they were more than happy to have her stay over.

Math, Biology, and English classes at Bella Vista Junior High dragged on like a line at the post office. Polly spent all her patience to sit through what seemed like the most boring three hours of her life. At lunch she marched directly to the cafeteria where she knew her friends would be waiting. She found them sitting at a table on the far side of the room and dropped onto the empty section of bench next to Alya.

"I feel like I'm crawling out of my skin waiting for this day to end. Psyche is out there, I know it. She could be dying in a ditch and I'm sitting here waiting through a lecture on how to cut up frogs and listening to the foundations of Middle English." Polly pushed her hands through her hair until her face tightened. Venting wasn't going to be enough.

"I know how you feel, but we have to wait it out. Another couple of hours won't make a difference." Alya's gaze drifted from Polly's face over to the window and through to the marsh next to their school.

"You know, Polly might be right." Bethany leaned over the table as she spoke. "If Psyche is injured, well, even an alien might suffer from exposure."

"We could still tell our parents. Or at least call nine-one-one again," Brittany's grave face unnerved Polly. If her most headstrong friend wanted to play it safe, they really had exhausted their options.

"And land Psyche in a hospital?" Polly's volume shot up and the freshmen at the table next to them turned to stare.

"If her monster bear really is dead, what harm would it do for Psyche to stay in bed a week or two?" Caroline adjusted her cardigan and looked around for more listeners.

"She seemed pretty sure our doctors would notice something different about her. Maybe they'd put her in a bed and let her sleep. Or maybe they'd take some blood and call the government with the results." Alya's words skittered across Polly's arms, causing tiny hairs to stand at attention.

"Either way, Psyche was pretty clear about not wanting to go. That should be enough for the rest of us. I mean, I believe her about the immortality stuff; I shouldn't say 'dying' like she's mortal. I guess I'm more worried that she's going to just up and pop back to her nebula on the other side of the universe. What's the life of one human woman compared to a timeless creature?" Polly stood abruptly. Her mind was made up. "I brought my bike to school. Nobody has to cut with me, but I'm leaving." Polly looked at Alya first, then at each of the others.

"You'll need someone to help you track her. Dammit." Alya scooped her books off the table.

"If she needs medical treatment, you have to promise we can call professionals. Who knows, our parents might help off the record." Bethany collected her books, too.

"I guess I still need to get you that key for my uncle's shop," Caroline sighed. "What better time—nobody's home."

"It's going to be worth it, guys. Mom is worth it." Polly's roiling nausea finally subsided. Everything was coming together. Everything *would* come together.

If they could just find Psyche.

Five bikes skidded to a halt on Polly's gravel driveway. Afternoon sun hit the bay window of her lifeless living room. Rounding the corner and seeing again the shredded wall and roof sent Polly's pulse racing even higher. She fought tears and swallowed yet another lump in her throat. She had so much left to deal with after they found Psyche. It would all have to wait, though. The girls scoured Polly's kitchen for food and would-be weapons, trading the books in their backpacks for trekking supplies once more.

"As soon as we get back to where those men shot the bear, I should be able to pick up a trail. It's going to be hard though—all those men traipsing around the orchard, as well as whoever else has wandered across the ground in the last day or so." Alya tied her hair back and adjusted the bag on her back.

Bethany and Brittany secured their own bags while Caroline retied her boots. Polly surveyed the damage to the west side of the house one more time.

"Did everyone manage to find some pennies or anything else made of copper?" A moment of doubt shook Polly like a change jar. Couldn't they offer Psyche some actual medicine? Or would that do more harm than good?

"I found some old wire in your garage," Brittany volunteered.

"This watering can looks like copper," said Caroline, producing a small pot from her bag.

Polly recognized the little can from the windowsill in the living room. It had been her grandmother's and her mom loved it. But would she trade it for a chance to beat cancer? Polly felt sure her mom would make that deal. "Yeah, I'm pretty sure it's copper. And I restocked with pennies from my piggy bank."

"I've got some, too," Bethany said. "Plus a ring from our trip to the copper mine in Spruce Valley." She held up a thick hammered band.

Polly sighed. "Let's get going then." They followed Alya then, heading out Polly's backyard and into the orchard.

The girls reached the disturbed patch of earth inside Lakeside Hills within half an hour. They watched, rapt with helpless tension as Alya studied the ground, walking around the marks and grooves, kneeling and crouching from various viewpoints. She finally made her way to the spot where Polly had found the scrunchie.

"It's a bit weird; I can't really explain it. There's a gap in her movement.

Like Psyche disappeared," Alya gestured at a spot a few feet behind her. "But I do see the deep, slanted footprints of someone running," she added, pointing at the ground beneath her feet. "I think she took off uphill, that way, back toward Polly's house."

"My place? Then why didn't we—" Recognition hijacked Polly's face. "The storage shed!" Polly took off at a hard run with her friends in immediate pursuit.

Minutes later they reached the old wood shack that had sheltered their strange friend twice now. Polly flung open the door. A blonde girl with creamy peach skin was slumped in the corner, wearing Polly's clothes but backwards. It wasn't Psyche. But it was.

Chapter 21

Tuesday morning brought them the dilemma of what to do with Psyche. Polly had decided to return home that night and take her chances with structural instability. Adding Psyche to the guest list at the Johnsons' would have been too complicated for everyone. Monday evening, once she was sure Psyche's memory had returned enough to function, Polly brought her up to speed on the death of Nur-gahl.

"You are unwise to believe that Nur-gahl is dead," Psyche said flatly. Polly paused, evaluating whether or not Psyche's tone showed any irritation.

"The parks officer, the police, and some other men that were all poking the dead bear's body were completely sure it was dead." Polly felt the tingling of adrenaline running through her limbs. She suddenly wondered how she herself had been so easily convinced.

"Psyche, we stuck around and grilled those men. Also, there haven't been any new attacks. Wouldn't Nur-gahl need to kill and feed on people to restore his strength? Or is he able to use metal the way you do? Even so, I think there would be some kind of hubbub in town if a dead bear walked out of the vet's and started a rampage. Again."

"Perhaps we could view his remains, as that officer had invited you to do?"

"Whatever it takes to keep you here a bit longer."

After feeding Psyche a dinner of frozen pizzas and diet cola, Polly convinced her guest to register as a student at Bella Vista Junior High. They would have two cover stories: for Polly's mom, Psyche was new in town with parents nearby; for the school, Psyche was an exchange student staying at Polly's house. The lies would hopefully not intersect, or need to hold up over a long period of time.

Polly had no reservations now about bringing Psyche to school. The latter's second attempt at becoming human had been much more successful. Without the stopover shift into a unicorn, Psyche's coloring had much more warmth. Her long hair was a pale, yellow shade of blonde, and her skin had a soft, peachy pink hue and seemed flawless. Her ice-blue eyes were more of a sapphire this time, although each and every facial feature and skeletal detail remained exactly the same. The effect was as if Psyche had simply washed off a translucent coat of white costume paint.

Polly stayed in the school office that morning, walking both the receptionist and Psyche through a barely credible account of how a Swedish exchange student—through the Girl Guides instead of the school—with no accent happened to be staying with her for the rest of the school year. In the end, Polly knew she hadn't sold the receptionist on their story, but she preferred to hide Psyche in plain sight, keeping her close.

The day flew past for Polly and her friends. All five girls had to serve detention over lunch hour for cutting classes the day before, but even that didn't dull their spirits. For Polly in particular, only one thought dominated her day: how soon could she get her hands on a pound of silver.

Three o'clock arrived. Polly escorted Psyche to the lawn next to the parking lot where they could wait for the school bus. Polly sensed eyes on them—more specifically, on Psyche. While her updated appearance had lost its standout characteristics, Psyche still looked very much like an undercover princess. Polly casually positioned herself between Psyche and a group of freshman boys who were staring a little too intently.

"I had a thought during Geography class that I feel compelled to share," Psyche said oblivious to her surroundings. "Given that you are correct about the administration woman not believing our explanation for my presence, will there not be a problem when the school attempts to contact your mother using the numerical code we gave them?" Psyche stood perfectly still, regarding Polly without blinking. Polly hadn't noticed it before, but Psyche never blinked.

"First of all, Mom is still in the hospital. Secondly, once I explain to Mom that your parents went back to Sweden for a funeral and couldn't take you, she'll insist you stay with us. I thought it over and unless the school happens to start grilling Mom about a fictitious exchange program, this really is a good cover story. I hate the circumstances, but realistically, Mom doesn't have the energy to dig up the truth about anything right now."

"I have noted the functional difference between 'parents' and 'mom.' Your other friends have a male adult in their homes. Where is yours?"

Polly's mouth hung open as she recovered from the verbal slug to the gut. Talking about her dad's death was almost unbearable now that her mom was sick. "I had one, but . . . Dad died in a car accident when I was six. I missed almost three months of school that year. It was the worst time in my life."

"Until now." Psyche looked at Polly with what seemed to be a stiff attempt at empathy. "Your mother's illness is additionally hard because after she passes you will be alone." Psyche paused, looking into Polly's eyes. "Your mother's sister is not available and you no longer have information for your father's family."

Polly took a deep, cleansing breath. "Do you see now why it's so important that Mom sticks around? I love her—that's most of it. But if she dies, I go god-knows-where. I can't sit back and take comfort from some abstract concept like her soul peacefully floating around the universe."

Psyche looked off into the overcast sky as though considering Polly's comment. At that moment their bus arrived and Polly guided Psyche to a seat at the back. They were lucky enough to have a few rows of empty seats ahead of them, —privacy for the drive to Lakeview Road.

"Polly, I still plan to heal your mom. But I understand a bit more now about what repercussions you will face in order to obtain the silver I need." Psyche spoke at regular volume. Polly felt her chest tighten.

"Shhhh. If anyone hears us talking about this, those 'repercussions' will stand a much bigger chance of coming to pass."

"I do not want you to take actions that will bring you unhappiness."

"Losing Mom is the greatest unhappiness that could ever happen to me. Read my mind. Look into my heart, or soul, or whatever." Polly's eyes bulged, her voice barely a whisper. "Unless I get caught in the act, I'll have the silver in your hands soon. And if it's not enough, tell me and I'll get more. We wait until Mom comes home from the hospital, which should be any day now. And then you heal her. Whatever happens after that doesn't matter to me in the slightest. Going to jail knowing Mom is alive would be a walk in the park."

Psyche regarded Polly for a long moment. "All right. We will coordinate with Caroline as soon as possible."

"Thank you, Psyche. This means everything to me."

Polly had forgotten, again, about the ruined state of her house until they got off the bus and she saw the debris still strewn on the lawn. But something else caught her eye as she and Psyche walked up the driveway. The crunch of gravel under their feet alerted Nick and his friend to their presence. The two boys were carrying a large roll of translucent plastic sheeting. Tool belts hung from their waists, clinking as they walked.

"Hey, Polly. I hope you don't mind—Ian and I thought you could use some help sealing off the damage here. I know your mom isn't able to chat with contractors right now and you can't very well sleep here with a giant hole in the side of the kitchen."

Tears pooled in Polly's eyes. "That is so incredibly thoughtful, Nick. Thank you. How did you know about this?"

"The twins told me. They thought I might be able to patch it up. I wish I had those skills. Maybe one day. Anyway, this won't be much of a fix, but it'll keep the elements out—for the most part." Nick smiled while adjusting the weight of the plastic roll. Ian grunted impatiently and Polly blushed. As soon as they left, Bethany and Brittany would be getting a phone call.

"Will you make another attempt to repair the damage properly at a later date?" Psyche asked in her usual deadpan tone.

Nick stared at her. "Uh, well, like I said, that's a pretty big job and I'm not nearly qualified enough to do it myself. I'm sure Mrs. Michaels will want to make arrangements for a professional. Once she's feeling better."

"Can we get you anything to eat?" Polly brightened at the chance to busy her hands.

"If you've got any sandwiches, we wouldn't turn you down," said Nick as he and Ian guided the roll to a spot on the patio.

"Consider it done!" Polly darted through the open wall. Psyche followed carefully, choosing her footing as she made her way through the mess of wood and glass.

Psyche stood next to Polly at the refrigerator door. "Is the dark-haired boy the one you have feelings for?"

"Wow, Psyche, you sure don't pull any punches." Polly set a jar of pickles and a packet of ham on the counter.

"I would never punch you, so there is no need to pull anything. I am merely observing that you have romantic emotions toward Nick. Perhaps you are not alone in the world after all? I remember you asking not to know what Nick thinks and feels. But if you change your mind, I can help." Psyche stood perfectly still a few feet behind Polly, who transferred a jar of mayonnaise and a bottle of mustard to her prep area.

"Okay, considering that you can read my mind anyway, I guess there's no hiding that I've got a crush. But that's all it is. Nick doesn't know. I don't *want* him to know. And even if he was the slightest bit interested—and to be crystal clear, you're right, I still don't want you to go digging in his head—I can't begin to think about a boyfriend until Mom is better. Does that make sense?"

"To you, I believe it does." Psyche remained motionless as Polly looked back.

"Psyche, why don't you go watch some television? Think of it as a study in human culture." Polly kept her eyes on the slices of bread in front of her.

"Why would I need to study your culture more than I already have? My mental records are full."

"So I can clear my head and make this food without cutting my thumb or accidentally slipping a layer of plastic wrap inside a sandwich."

"All right." Psyche retreated to the living room with her unnaturally silent grace.

"How are those sandwiches coming?" Nick asked a few minutes later, entering the kitchen from the living room. He and Ian had finished sealing off the wall where the sliding glass door had been.

"It's not much, but they're ready. I hope you like ham and cheese." Polly handed two plates to Nick while Ian waited awkwardly on the back patio.

"I love ham and cheese. I'm sure Ian does, too. He's just playing shy. Probably on account of your new friend there." Nick smirked and Polly blushed again.

"Psyche is . . . not from around here." Polly clasped her hands with nervous vigor.

"I remember her coming into the hardware store with you. Where is she from?" Nick set both plates on the kitchen table, picked up one half of his sandwich and took a bite. Polly got a small kick out of his willingness to leave Ian hanging. "I've gotta say, you look a lot better than you did the other day," Nick added, speaking to Psyche directly as she re-entered the kitchen.

"My home is very far from here."

"Sweden. She's an exchange student staying with me for a while." The information tumbled quickly out of Polly. She looked at Psyche. "And she had a stomach bug over the weekend. But it's really good timing that she's here. Now that Mom's back in the hospital, I would have been stuck here on my own."

"That's a good point. Polly, I have no idea how you've been keeping it together, but I hope this all works out. I really do." Nick finished the first half of his sandwich and picked up both plates again. "I better go feed Ian before he passes out. We'll be out of your hair in a few minutes."

Nick let himself out the front door. Polly watched as he marched briskly past the living room window. A few beats later he was back with Ian on the other side of the thick milky utility plastic. They ate and mumbled to one another, seeming generally uncomfortable.

"I'll seal this properly when they leave," Psyche said calmly.

Polly was getting used to the strange things that came out of Psyche's mouth. Since it didn't seem to be much of a liability, considering that a whole wall had already been trashed, Polly figured she'd step aside and let Psyche do her thing.

Chapter 22

Polly confirmed that Nick's pickup truck had pulled away from the curb out front before nodding to Psyche, who made her way around to the patio. Polly followed, fascinated and a little giddy. The guys had taken their tools, so Psyche didn't have so much as a staple gun to work with. What could she possibly be planning to do?

Psyche held out her arms. Polly thought for a beat that her strange friend was focusing telekinetic energy, as she'd seen her do before. Blue light erupted from Psyche's fingertips, crackling, a growing orb that surrounded both hands. Polly remembered then—the electrical storm she had seen over the orchard that night. The balls of electrostatic energy growing in front of Psyche shot out in two arcs, each striking the edges of the plastic sheeting. Psyche moved the energy quickly, letting it touch barely long enough to melt the edges of the plastic into the wood siding of the house. Acrid fumes wafted back at them, and the charge around Psyche's hands snapped off like someone had hit a switch. It had been mere seconds, but the plastic seal was now taut and airtight.

"When the hell did you learn to do THAT?"

"When I returned to this dimension after attempting to maroon Nur-gahl, I shifted once and properly. You have noticed my newfound success with this body. It is because I had memory of human form, so my essence was better able to generate human cells. And to execute my physical abilities as intended." Psyche leaned forward to evaluate the plastic wall. "I am at full strength now, complete with my entire range of energy control. And that is what Nur-gahl wants from me. He knows that consuming a fellow morphling will allow him to take on new traits. Command of electricity is minor, though; it is my ability to slice into spacetime that is unique, now that only two morphlings remain. It is why I can open gateways and he cannot."

"Now I get why you look more . . . human. But Nur-gahl travels, too. How is he doing that?" Polly's attention transferred from the plastic to Psyche's facial features.

"Nur-gahl travels by slipping into my wake and using the portals I create. It is not hard for our kind to detect a fissure opening nearby. As long as he does not stray too far from my location, he can slip through shortly after I have gone."

"What do you mean by shortly?"

"Roughly two of your seconds."

"That long, eh?" As soon as she spoke, Polly knew her sarcasm was lost on Psyche.

"If you remember my earlier explanation, the trouble is not manipulating whether or not he follows me. The challenge is finding somewhere I can safely maroon him for eternity. Or I must crush him with the closure of a fissure, but that is unlikely. No, I have to be certain there is no other life left on any plane where I leave Nur-gahl forever. I had it last time. My energy was drawn by an isolated endling that died as I entered that realm. And Nur-gahl followed me to his doom. But when I left, he was able to follow me again. It was only by sheer luck that some of your adult hunters attacked him after he re-entered this world. Still, I was foolish to think I could slip back here. I knew I had to keep my word to you though, so I will uphold my vow and defeat Nur-gahl again. Next time, I will not be foolish enough to think I can retreat. I will remain with his essence as long as I must, even until the end of the universe."

"It doesn't matter now, does it? He's dead—I saw his body. Those men were sure." Polly spoke frantically, panic and doubt seeping into her.

"No. He is not dead. I can tell how badly you want it to be true, but you and those men are mistaken." Psyche's placid face sent a shiver of fear through Polly's heart.

"What do you mean? He's been dead for days now. He wouldn't just lay there like a corpse in some vet's cold storage."

"That is exactly his plan. He was wounded quite grievously by gunshots immediately after he followed me back. To Nur-gahl, the refrigeration you mentioned is a golden opportunity to heal in peace."

"But what about Mom? Are you still going to help her? Or are you going back to hunting Nur-gahl?" Polly's insides tensed.

"We have time. You have done everything in your power to assist me. And you have put yourself in peril for my cause. I believe that you will do so again, for your mother, in order to procure the silver I need. I can think of no creature more deserving of a boon."

Polly let the air out of her lungs. A sob caught in her throat and she sprang a hug on Psyche—their first, Polly realized as she clung to a body that was both slender and strong as iron.

"I'll call Caroline right away." Polly reached for the door and recoiled when her hands grazed plastic. She laughed and skipped around to the front of the house.

Polly was already talking on the phone when Psyche sat down carefully in the Michaels' living room. Polly hung up a moment later. "Let's celebrate with some music!" she said and scooped the remote off the coffee table. She pointed it at the television and switched to Much Music. She squealed with delight as Pat Benatar appeared singing *"We are strong!"* while sneering at a father figure.

"I love this song!" Polly shouted as she turned up the volume.

Psyche tilted her head, a confused frown settling on her face while Polly bounced around the room. "This woman on the screen is leaving her family behind. Her life appears harder. She looks lost even with people around. Why does this make you feel empowered?"

Polly belted out *"We are young!"* in tune with the video, completely ignoring Psyche.

"How are they defeating that man by shaking their chests at him?"

"You're missing the point, Psyche!"

Psyche shook her head. Polly danced along, copying the choreographed routine. A new video started—a graffitied door opening onto a concrete corridor. Psyche's interest was renewed.

"This is Joy Division. Also awesome!" Polly said as she stopped to catch her breath. She turned the volume down slightly, the more soothing tune calming her mood.

"Love does tear people apart," said Psyche knowingly.

"That's a bit heavy for a Monday," said Brittany, and Polly jumped. Psyche turned to look.

"Where did you come from!" Polly exclaimed, hand on her heart.

"My charming sister talked Nick into slapping a bandage on your broken house. I wanted to make sure he actually did it." Brittany smiled as she chewed a wad of gum. She blew a large pink bubble.

"He did. And why exactly did you think that was a good idea?" Polly glowered.

Bethany appeared then with Alya in tow.

"You won't have random creatures wandering in from the hills, for a start." Brittany snapped her gum.

"Okay, you checked on me. But I could barely feed Nick and Ian, so I hope you can make it home in time for dinner."

"I brought food," Caroline added as she joined the room, bags from her parents' restaurant in each hand.

"Normally I'd love having people over, but I don't want more attention on this place than absolutely necessary right now. Mom could come home any moment. Your parents probably all know about the damage and they'll be worried. Maybe enough to come here and poke around. I just can't afford for Psyche to be found out in case they take her away." Fear infused Polly's words.

"We're helping you, and your mom, whether our parents like it or not," said Alya.

"And no one is taking anyone anywhere." Bethany put her hand on Polly's shoulder.

Polly relented and hugged each of them in turn.

"That's more like it," Alya said. "Now let's get down to business."

"I'm going to Valley Hardware after this to get a copy of my uncle's key. He's back at work tomorrow and I need to return the original before he notices it's gone." Caroline held up a simple shiny steel key for all to observe.

"Are you sure that's a good idea? What if Valley Hardware keeps records? What if they ask what the key opens or who owns it?" Polly's words tumbled out of her like water from a hose.

"What if Nick sees you?" Brittany stopped chewing and gave Polly a sly smile.

Psyche carefully took the key from Caroline's hand and picked up a few coins from the dish on the coffee table.

"Are you . . . hungry again?" Bethany eyed Psyche for signs of distress.

Psyche closed her left hand over Caroline's key and her right on the coins. Blue light escaped through the cracks in her fingers—it lasted only a moment before fading again. She opened both hands to reveal two matching keys.

"Bitchin'!" shouted Brittany.

"Cool!" exclaimed Alya.

"Wicked!" said Bethany.

Polly and Caroline exchanged startled looks that melted into smiles. Then:

"What are you girls up to in here?"

Polly's mom called from the front door. She hefted a bag over the threshold and smiled at the group.

Chapter 23

Polly darted over to her mom and gave her a quick hug before scooping the nylon overnight bag into her arms.

"I see you girls sealed off that disaster on the side of the house. Thank you for taking care of that. Between your help and Mrs. Johnson coming by to bring me some clothes, this latest hospital stay wasn't that bad." Mom smiled weakly. A wave of sadness struck Polly's chest.

"We had help. It looked a bit wonky at first, but in the end, we got a surprisingly good seal." Polly glanced at Psyche.

"It is Polly's friend Nick and the other boy, Ian, who deserve recognition, Ms. Michaels."

"I'll have to take them some muffins as soon as I'm up for it. And Mrs. Johnson tells me that crazy wild bear was shot. You girls weren't too close when it happened, I hope." Mom dropped heavily into her cozy armchair.

"We heard the shots, but that was it." Polly and the girls exchanged nervous glances, but Mom had already closed her tired eyes.

"Caroline brought some dinner. Can we make you a plate Ms. Michaels?" Bethany volunteered and her sister nodded.

"I'll get it started," said Caroline.

"I'll help tidy the kitchen. It's the least we can do," added Alya, trotting off after Caroline and the twins.

"Mom, is it okay if Psyche spends the night again? Her parents are still out of town and will be for a while longer." Polly stood on her toes with both hands clasped behind her back.

"I see you still haven't learned how to pronounce your friend's name properly." Mom opened her eyes and gave Polly a mildly disapproving stare.

"It was my idea, Ms. Michaels. My parents are Scandinavian—very traditional. But I wanted a nickname that my new friends would not stumble over."

"If you don't mind my saying, Psyche, your English is quite good. I can't pick up even a hint of an accent." Mom smiled at Psyche who replied in kind.

"She's settling in pretty smoothly." Polly crossed her arms casually. "We'd better go help the girls with dinner now," she added, beckoning for Psyche to follow. The smell of braised meat was already wafting through the house.

The next morning, the beige stucco of Bella Vista Junior High beamed under a blue sky. A beautiful balmy day gave the girls an easy excuse to gather on the bleachers next to the baseball diamond.

"We still need to speak quietly out here. You never know how sound is going to carry," Caroline said as she leaned in to the huddle, cradling her well-loved biology textbook. She set the book down along with a clear plastic folder containing her extra credit mitosis project.

"Anyone who sees us sitting out here is only going to think we're gossiping." Bethany laid back on the stretch of bleacher beside her. She donned her mirror finish sunglasses, rested her arms on her belly, and let the sun bathe her face. Farther down the bench, Brittany copied her sister's pose—they looked completely identical in their glasses, acid wash jeans, and trendy black t-shirts with a layer of fishnet overtop.

"You got the key back to your uncle with no problem?" Polly whispered at Caroline.

"I think so. If he was missing it, he never said anything to my parents—not in front of me. He lives in our basement suite, so if he'd been freaking out, I would have heard about it."

"What's the best time to do it?" Alya asked, nodding toward downtown.

"He's usually at the shop late doing inventory the last Friday of every month. They take a shipment a day or so before. That's when they've got the most stock."

"Unless a tour bus comes in and decides to all buy silver trinkets." Brittany lifted her head to see if she'd gotten a rise out of anyone. Bethany looked up and pulled down her sunglasses to glare at her sister.

"I'm trying to be serious here." Caroline glowered at the twins. "My Uncle also keeps a small amount of sterling silver sheet metal and wire for doing repair work. I overheard him telling my dad the other day that he's tired of having to bring in those supplies because the price is always changing and he doesn't want to do repairs anymore. It's time consuming and customers are too picky. This is probably the last time he'll get a big order of silver for a long time."

Polly sat up straight, suddenly struck by an idea. "Psyche, if you can open portals within our world without scrambling your brain, could you slip in and out of Sun Valley at night? We wouldn't need that key. No one would be the wiser."

"Every time I use energy," Psyche said while staring serenely at a cloud, "be it to move an object or to control current, I must replenish and recharge myself. You will be best served in the immediate future by my saving my strength for your mother."

"I'd feel better if it was just you, Polly. But if two go in, I want you at least present. No offence, Psyche." Caroline cast an apologetic look between both girls. "And I think it has to be Friday night, as late as possible to be sure nobody is still there counting anything."

"Psyche, can you cut power to an alarm without burning up too much of your energy?" Polly waved her fingers, mimicking Psyche's powers. Psyche contemplated the question while pressing down on the gland in her palm. She nodded.

"Okay, good," Caroline said. "I know there's also a safe, which most stuff will be locked inside. All the counters and cabinets are locked, too. And there's a camera, but I think I've seen where they shut it off. You'll need to go to the desk in the back room."

Polly saw the fear in Caroline's eyes and sensed tightness throughout her body. The exterior of the town police hall sprang to mind, complete with the small granite fountain out front. Polly had never been inside—she didn't know if the building even had jail cells. She felt a pang of remorse then at coercing her friend into what she finally appreciated as being a serious crime. But she forced the emotion back down, through her belly and into nothingness. This was about her mom's *life*. Unless she stopped believing in Psyche's abilities—which wasn't going to happen—the consequences of getting caught were still preferable to not trying.

"I know everyone here wants to help, but this isn't a five-person job." Polly stood up and took a step back. "It isn't even a three-person job. Caroline, I don't want you within a mile of the shop when this happens. And Psyche, I can't stress enough how much it means to me that you can do this. I know you can see and hear inside my head, but I can't do the same, so you'll have to let me say the words out loud: Thank you."

"We have not succeeded yet. Thank me when the task is complete." Psyche rose and stood next to Polly.

"So, that's it then. I guess the rest of us need to make sure we've got alibis." Brittany grinned at her sister and at each of the girls in the circle. Polly relaxed and sat back down, so Psyche did the same.

"I have an additional requirement." Psyche's smile melted, revealing a cold, stoic face in its place.

"And that is?" Polly asked warily.

"The same as it was before. We need to completely destroy Nur-gahl."

Brittany let out a loud, exasperated breath. "Wait, what? That bear is dead. We were there." Bethany shushed her sister with a shove. "Clearly we were wrong."

"Assuming your battle with him, and the hunters' gunshots that followed, were not enough to kill this thing, how on Earth do you expect *us*"—Alya gestured rapidly between herself, Polly, and the rest, "to finish it off?"

"Do you remember telling us that one of your people could absorb another? Is that really not an option for you?" Bethany did her best to keep her tone respectful.

Psyche shuddered and shook her head.

"That's a 'no' then. So, you want to try burning the body?" Brittany said, one eyebrow cocked.

"For a start, I would like to be sure that his body is in fact still there. And if it is, I will use the salt we procured before, and yes, I will incinerate his remains. From there, I will attempt to reconnect to the barren realm and force his essence through. My having traveled there should make up for not being drawn by a life force. If fate is on our side, we will find Nur-gahl before he is able to recover and defeating him will be attainable. And then we will take the silver needed to heal Polly's mother."

"This is all for real now, eh?" Alya lifted her glasses and massaged the bridge of her nose.

"Sounds like it. The next sensible thing to do is to make sure we're all seen out together on Friday night. Polly and Psyche can slip away and come back. We'll all be ready to cover for them if anyone asks," said Bethany.

"Let's do it at the Rack Shack. The place will be busy—loads of people will see us." Brittany rubbed her hands together eagerly. The fishnet layer of her shirt moved hypnotically. Polly wondered whether her friend's enthusiasm was going to be a blessing or a curse.

"What is a 'Rack Shack'?" Psyche asked curiously.

"It's a pool hall," answered Polly.

"More importantly, Brittany is right. We won't need alibis if we're seen in there on Friday night. Losing track of someone in there is to be expected. But still, Polly and Psyche shouldn't be gone for too long. Otherwise this whole plan could backfire," said Bethany.

The school's bell rang in the distance and echoed across the field. The girls all rose out of instinctive obedience to the sound.

"That's a good point. Although it's nice to have this mostly sorted out now." Caroline hugged her book and folder.

"We should make a point of keeping to ourselves until Friday. No hanging out with anyone extra, friends or strangers, who might want to make other plans or join us," Alya said as they stomped down the metal bleachers.

"And once we're inside the Rack Shack, we play pool among ourselves; no games for other people's tables or quarters or any of that," added Bethany, adjusting her lopsided fishnet layer.

"If it's too busy, we'll just grab a counter on the back wall and eat fries. We'll still be seen," said Caroline.

"I've got one more thought." Polly stopped in front of her friends. "What if we go to this vet's place and the bear's body isn't there? Maybe they've cremated it by now. Not finding it doesn't mean that thing came back to life and ran off." Polly focused on Psyche as they crossed the lawn back toward the school.

"In that event, I will be able to detect evidence of his demise, do not fear."

"I think what we're afraid of is having to deal with that demon bear again," Alya whispered as the group neared the side entrance.

"You are quite right to worry," said Psyche as the girls passed through the doors. They clenched their mouths within the bustle of students hurrying to classes.

Chapter 24

Wednesday and Thursday crawled along at the speed of paint drying. All Polly's teachers sounded like partially muted static.

Summer seemed to have changed its mind about inhabiting Bella Vista. Overcast skies drizzled through unseasonably chilly days, forcing Polly to revert to her spring fleece jacket. Polly found herself telling Psyche over and over how beautiful Bella Vista would be soon. How wonderful beach life was around the town's three lakes. Psyche humored Polly each time, never once reminding her that summer was irrelevant for someone who'd be departing the planet—possibly even the entire dimension—in a few days' time.

"So what are we going to do tonight? We have to think of something. All this hurry-up-and-wait is driving me completely insane!" Polly said to Psyche as they walked to her house, their school bus rumbling away from the intersection.

"We could meditate."

"You want to what now? After everything we've been through this week? You're about to leave forever and all you want to do is sit around cross-legged and hum?" Polly shoved wavy red locks out of her face and the wind put them right back.

"I have absolutely no intention of humming. Yet we should sit. With our bodies. We will need to be safe and comfortable once we depart astrally."

Psyche stopped walking and looked up at the gray clouds tumbling quickly overhead.

Polly adjusted her backpack and tucked her arms close to her body. The wind made her uncomfortable and she wanted to get home as quickly as possible. Still, she summoned as much fortitude as she could muster and backtracked to where Psyche stood, unaffected, at the side of the road next to a row of wild yellow daisies.

"I'm past the point of asking whether or not you're for real, but Psyche . . ."

"My race is not capable, nor interested in, anything as messy and painful as love. I do enjoy your company, Polly, and I will somewhat regret never seeing you again. I would like you to have an experience that will help you remember me. It is something no other of your kind has ever seen." Psyche's face tilted down. She gazed at Polly, almost tenderly.

"What it is you want me to see?"

"My home." Psyche's mouth cracked into an awkward smile.

They waited until Polly's mom had gone to bed, which was not long after sunset. Psyche suggested the living room for their mediation. Polly wanted to hide in her room, but Psyche explained that the house's largest room, with the most glass, was their best starting point.

"So how do we do this? I'm not even sure I can do that feet-on-the-knees pose you see in movies."

"Your species has such rigid visualization skills," said Psyche, shaking her head. "I will sit comfortably on your couch. You sit next to me. Repeat what I say. Follow my instructions."

"Fair enough." Polly sat next to her.

Psyche rubbed her hands together, beckoning Polly to do the same. Psyche then massaged her face. Polly copied her. Psyche grunted. Polly did that, too, glancing upstairs, listening for signs of movement from her mom. Nothing.

More rubbing and grunting led to Psyche taking several deep breaths, each time blowing out vigorously. She stopped, sat back, and remained stone still.

Polly scanned the room for some sign of change. Psyche stayed motionless for a moment that seemed to stretch into the distance as a blustery night clawed at the siding and shutters. Polly was ready to stand and declare a stop to the nonsense when Psyche's slender hand turned over, inviting Polly to clasp.

Polly took Psyche's cold hand in hers and waited. After a while she decided it really was time to back off and give the morphling some time alone. She opened her eyes and stood up—at least she thought she did. Darkness clung to her like smoke. Cotton filled her ears as she walked forward across uneven ground. A faint light coming from somewhere far ahead glinted with millions of tiny dots spread out across the ground. It looked as though she was walking across the bottom of a cavern. She put one foot in front of the other until the blackness around her started to fade. Ancient stars silently poked their heads through a plum taffeta curtain that seemed to billow with a subtle shimmer. Polly noticed Psyche standing nearby, observing everything with indifferent wisdom. It was then that Polly realized: they were inside Psyche's home nebula—they were in another dimension.

The ground beneath them evened out, smooth and flat and lustrous. It looked like marble, although Polly couldn't be sure. Ahead of her, the outline of a table solidified. She could make out two pedestal seats positioned on either side. Polly sensed Psyche beside her. Together they went over to the table.

"This place is amazing, Psyche. It's breathtaking. It's epic. It's—"

"Home. And I'm sure you see it a little differently than I do. Remember, Polly, there is nothing physical in this place. Whatever you see under you, around you, across from you—none of this is 'here' in the way *you* define that word." As Psyche finished speaking, Polly focused on her face, trying to get a clearer look at Psyche's profile in the dim light.

Polly's heart wrenched as Psyche's face flickered and evaporated into colorful smoke. Opalescent mist, shimmering with every subtle color of the rainbow floated up and around and back to where Psyche had been sitting. Her chair was gone. The table, too, in a blink.

A soft meadow of mossy grass rested beneath her feet as though it had always been there. Polly watched the horizon as a hint of blue light erupted into a sunrise, impossibly transforming the vast expanse of space into a terrestrial sky.

"On the subject of being here, do not be too frightened. I can feel tension in you. You are not really in the Astral Temple. You are in a place we can visit together, like a gap in the wall between my world and yours."

Polly reached out to touch the mist that hovered in front of her. The opal haze retreated from her fingertips and condensed as it took the shape of a horse. Polly knew even before the edges came into focus what was coming.

Psyche faced Polly now as a unicorn, crowned with a devastatingly beautiful pearl-colored horn.

"You must never forget that I am not, nor was I ever, another human girl. I was never a unicorn either. I have existed before the dust and rock of your world spun together to birth a planet. I care for you, but you must understand that I cannot stay in your realm. To do so would be to forget my purpose: I am the last guardian of my people's vast repository of universal knowledge."

"I get it. I do. You're like an ancient goddess and I'm kind of like a . . . muskrat or some primitive mammal. I wouldn't hang out with an ant on an anthill for long either." Polly ached to run her fingers through the unicorn's hair, or to lay a single finger on that horn. A small voice inside her head reminded her that no part of the unicorn was really there.

"It is time to go now."

"I know. I'm ready."

Chapter 25

On Friday night, Polly's mom dropped Polly and Psyche off just around the corner from the Rack Shack. To Ms. Michaels, it was routine. To Polly, it was the most important night of her life.

The girls turned the corner onto Bella Vista's main street and a gust of wind hit them head on, sending their hair twirling like horsetails—one the red-orange of a sunset, the other like sun-bleached wheat. Their eyes were decorated with a light dusting of green and blue respectively—lashes coated with mascara, much to Psyche's dislike.

Polly hiked up the collar of her denim jacket, careful not to smudge her cherry lips. Psyche copied her, gingerly shielding her own pink gloss. Polly instructed Psyche to casually, and in her own time, copy as many of her gestures as felt natural. Psyche's inherent stillness might draw attention to their group once inside the Rack Shack; their plan to be seen but not scrutinized could go sideways quickly.

As they got closer, they picked up the vibration and muffled sounds of pop music coming from the pool hall. The girls caught the attention of a group of kids out front. Polly recognized one of them right away.

"Hey, Polly," Nick's friend, Ian, sneered at her. His expression looked drained under the fluorescent light of the Rack Shack's sign. The scowl on his face wasn't helping much. Polly was struck wondering what it was Nick saw in Ian as a friend.

"Hi, Ian. Thanks again for helping me and my mom with that damage control." Polly put extra effort into her grateful tone. Ian's face remained the same.

"Who's your friend here?" he asked, stepping away from his group. He lifted the brim of his ball cap, shoved his bangs back, and pulled the hat down.

"This is Psyche. I'm sorry I didn't introduce you yesterday. I guess I'm still rattled from the whole bear-attacked-my-house thing." Polly shifted from one foot to the other. The night air and Ian's glassy eyes left her chilled to the bone. "Well, I guess we better head inside. I'm freezing out here!"

"Nick and I stopped to see my grandparents on our way home from your place. I told them about your friend." Ian's gaze shifted, latching on to Psyche.

"Oh? Are they thinking of hosting an exchange student, too?" Polly's stomach started to shrink.

"No. They had a run-in with a girl last week that kind of put them off the whole helping strangers thing. Some homeless albino girl, our age they think, broke into their backyard, stole my grandma's clothes, and attacked my grandpa with some kinda chemical weapon. If I didn't know you, Polly, I'd be taking a hard look at your pale blonde friend here."

"Psyche? No way. She wouldn't hurt a fly much less steal anything." Polly stepped between Ian and Psyche. "Either way, you can see Psyche isn't albino. She's Scandinavian; Swedish, specifically. That's a pretty big difference."

Polly was torn between talking Ian out of his suspicions and just moving along to keep their plan on track. She was still uneasy about the uncertain variables of their situation—an undead demon bear and a small-town jeweler's security. If the police came looking for Psyche after she skipped town, they might take an interest in her instead—something Polly wanted to avoid if possible.

"Bella Vista is a small town. There's nobody else like your friend around here, much less an albino *and* a Swedish girl both appearing on Lakeview Road." Ian craned his neck around Polly, trying to get a better look at Psyche's face.

Psyche returned Ian's gaze. Her stony expression did not put Ian or Polly at ease.

"Ian, I don't know what to say. I'm really grateful to you and Nick for your help the other day. But Psyche didn't do anything. Not to your grandparents or anyone else. I did call nine-one-one last weekend because I saw what I thought was an injured girl in the orchard. Psyche isn't the girl I saw. I can promise you that."

Polly locked her arm into Psyche's and tugged her toward the Rack Shack's front door.

"Pretty weird name if you ask me." Ian wasn't satisfied but still took a step back.

"Tell me about it. Well, have fun tonight." Polly rushed Psyche through the bodies loitering at the entrance. Pounding rock beats overwhelmed them. Polly glanced back to see Ian retreat to his friends while still watching the back of Psyche's head.

"Polly!" Brittany exclaimed from a table set against the wall, toward the back of the main level, just like they'd planned. Polly gave a small wave. Psyche did the same, but hers looked more like a salute. Polly sighed. All that raw data in Psyche's head and still so many human social subtleties didn't translate in practice.

"Hey, guys." Polly shrugged off her jacket and draped it over a chair.

"What were you talking to Ian about outside?" Alya set her pool cue on the table and leaned in to make her voice heard.

"We saw you through the window. He looked very unhappy," said Caroline, also shouting over the music.

"Oh, nothing," said Polly.

"That is not true, Polly. Your friend is aware of the incident I experienced after my first entry to your world." Psyche spoke even more loudly, to be heard over the music. Polly gave her a wide-eyed look of alarm. The twins added their heads to the circle with intense interest.

"Not that it matters now, but it looks like Ian's grandparents are the ones with a chunk missing from their back fence." Polly nervously re-glossed her lips.

"Ah. And they can pick Psyche out of a lineup?" asked Brittany, propping herself up with her pool cue.

"Not now. Her updated look should put a stop to that," said Polly, giving Psyche a final once-over.

"Ian did not seem to think my pigment change would prevent his grandparents from identifying me; however, you are correct that it is a moot point." Psyche sat with perfect posture on a swivel stool next to the wall counter. The bearings in the seat responded, startling Psyche as she moved unexpectedly. She overcorrected one way, then another, and to her delight, twisted back and forth. Polly burst with laughter and a fit of giggles overtook the rest of them.

"Wow, I needed that! It feels so good to laugh." Polly dried tears from the corner of her eyes.

"I hate to be a downer, but … are we still a go for . . . the thing?" Bethany asked, whipping her ponytail around as she looked at the faces of her friends.

"Hey, I've done my bit. Anything more and I won't be able to sleep at night." Caroline held her hands up, eyebrows raised.

"Don't feel guilty. You did what you did for a good cause," said Bethany.

"This time tomorrow you'll feel much better," Brittany said to Caroline. To the rest of them, she added, "And we shouldn't let a snarky dork like Ian spook us." Brittany leaned back and shot a dirty look at Ian's profile, visible through the front window. Polly frowned at Brittany and furiously waved her back into the huddle.

"This little conference, what we're doing right now, is exactly the kind of suspicious crap we should be avoiding," Polly said, glaring at Brittany again. She picked Alya's pool cue up off the table and, blocking out the mumbling conversation coming from her friends, concentrated on the beats thumping out of the speakers overhead. She lined up a shot. *Just for kicks, guide this in if you can,* she thought, directing it at Psyche. "Number two in the left back corner." Polly shouted before she took the shot. The cue ball barely hit its target, which in turn veered in the wrong direction. Then the two ball broke the laws of physics and curved its way into the hole.

"What the hell kind of shot was that!" shouted Brittany.

Polly offered the cue to Alya again. "Nah," she said, waving it off. "I think you can take it from here." Alya's mouth slid into a wry smile.

"Great, we're just going to let them cheat?" Brittany cocked her thumb between Polly and Psyche.

"I'm not cheating. I took a shot. It went in," Polly lied. Psyche's face remained steadfast.

"You have to admit, you've always been comfortable with breaking rules," said Alya, crossing her arms at Polly.

"If you don't get caught, are you really breaking a rule?" Polly took another shot. The ball dropped into the corner pocket. She wondered if she had made that shot with her own skill.

"Rules are rules, Polly. The only reason we're with you tonight is for Mrs. Michaels. My parents don't like me coming here at all and I have lots of chemistry homework this weekend. I need a high A in that class just to set things right in my head." Caroline straightened her cream cable knit sweater and smoothed down her pleated plaid skirt.

"As long as it gets the job done, I'm not picky about anyone's motives." Polly cracked another shot. She missed the side pocket and glared at Psyche.

"You did not ask for help." Psyche tilted her head, unblinking.

"Ha!" blurted Brittany. "I knew it."

Polly shrugged her shoulders and smiled. "Do you remember when we started hanging out?" She waited a beat for emphasis, not responses. "I do. We called it playing. That's how long we've been friends." Polly rested the butt of her cue on the ground and leaned on it as Brittany was doing.

"Now you're stalling," said Bethany. Polly smiled and handed the pool cue to Alya, who sighed and reluctantly lined up a shot.

"It's important for us to remember who we are to each other. Most girls change friends and crowds all the time. And that's fine for them. But we've been friends since kindergarten. The more time that passes, the more our friendship means. You guys were there for me when Dad died. Alya, remember when your dad lost his job and you had nothing but peanut butter sandwiches in your lunch for months? We all shared our food. Caroline, do you remember when the city shut down your parents' restaurant for a month over a stupid complaint? We all made sure you got clothes from our closets when your mom couldn't buy you anything. We've had hard times and we've been there for each other. I know tonight is a big ask." Polly paused to scan the area around them, to see if anyone was paying attention to them. "That's why it's just me and Psyche doing 'the thing.' But I appreciate everything you are all doing."

The music died down. Chatter filled the void until the electronic sounds of Dire Straits blasted from the wall-mounted speakers across the room.

"Polly, I believe it is time to go." Psyche stood and stepped to Polly's side.

"So . . . wish us luck, ladies." Polly picked up her jacket but didn't put it on. "Psyche, we're going out the back door. Girls, give us an hour and check to make sure the stopper is still wedged beneath the door. If we're lucky, people will just think I've been in the bathroom for way too long." Polly pursed her lips, looked at each of her friends for courage, and turned to leave.

"Polly," Caroline called out. Polly turned around. "Good luck!"

Polly saw Caroline's hand move, then drop, as she fought the urge to wave.

Chapter 26

"Now remember, it's the Sun Valley Jeweler's we have a key for, not the vet's office. I'm not really worried about the latter though, because I don't have a friend sticking her neck out to get us in there." Polly hugged her body as she marched. The night was cool, made downright cold by the wind. Psyche appeared still unaffected by the temperature as she walked next to Polly with calm, willowy strides.

"You are less concerned about the vet as we do not need to conceal our intrusion. That makes sense. When we reach the building housing Nur-gahl, I should be able to pull open a door or window telekinetically. I can destroy the circuitry of any alarm by overloading the system. The damage will be obvious, so we should work quickly. If we encounter another person in the process, I have one more trick at my disposal." Psyche raised her fingertips and re-tested the effectiveness of her ability to generate and manipulate her distinctive blue electricity. "You should be aware that if we draw attention, and I am required to defend you, my powers are capable of causing serious injury to humans. Although I sense you understand that already." Psyche looked ghostly as she and Polly passed under a streetlight.

"Yeah, I couldn't care less about the vet discovering a break-in, as long as we're not there when it happens. We also need to worry about not leaving evidence behind at Sun Valley. They will discover that someone stole from them, there's no way around that, but we can't let this come back to Caroline in any way." Polly's gaze zipped around in all directions. They turned onto the quiet side street where Bella Vista's only veterinarian was located. There was not a soul in sight.

Lake Country Veterinary was a renovated single-floor home with a wood sign on the lawn. The building and sign were dark, not intended to be visited at night. Polly and Psyche reached the edge of the property before spying a shattered front door. Only half the doorjamb remained, surrounded by crumbling stucco.

"Oh. My. God." Polly slapped her hand over her mouth.

"I think we can conclude that Nur-gahl is alive." Psyche's gentle words had none of the I-told-you-so mocking another girl might have employed, but Polly felt the urge to snap at her all the same.

"It could be a coincidence."

"You already know that is unlikely."

"Let's check anyway."

"Of course."

Psyche followed Polly down the sidewalk and up the front steps. They saw the entrance in more detail. Polly gasped. Cracks ran up and around what was left of the doorjamb. Massive slash marks on the entryway's wall testified to the structure's encounter with an angry wild animal.

The wailing of sirens erupted from the center of town.

Polly let out the breath she'd been holding for too long. "Oh great. Cops. We need to get out of here. Like, now!" She grabbed Psyche's arm and they ran back out onto the front porch just as a Bella Vista PD patrol car screeched around the corner, bright red and blue flashing from its roof.

"Shit!" Polly yanked Psyche back into the vet's waiting room and started desperately searching for another way out. A patio door that led out back beckoned her from across the kitchen.

"Did they see us? Listen to their minds!" Polly hissed.

Psyche was silent as Polly dragged her through the patio door and into the backyard behind the clinic.

"They are aware that someone is in this house. They are confused. And very afraid."

Polly ran to the fence at the back of the yard. Piles upon piles of wire cages blocked access to the gate. Trees in the alley taunted her, waving supple leafy branches in the night.

"We can't be caught here! Psyche, help!" Desperation poured from Polly's heart and out through her mouth as tears spilled from her eyes.

Psyche put one hand on Polly's shoulder and with her other launched the cages sideways with a single sweep. Relief propelled Polly through the gate and around the corner to where she hid beside a garbage can, panting. Psyche slipped out and crouched beside her.

"We should not remain here. We are not far enough from discovery. The policemen are searching the house. Both plan to move to the backyard in seconds. Walk slowly. Running will draw attention." Psyche walked casually through the alley. Polly hurried to her side.

"Right, I get it. We could have been simply walking through the alley. They never saw us on the property. It'll be easy to convince them some rough guys just ran past us." Polly wrung her hands, speaking mostly to herself.

"You are correct. We do not match the images in the policemen's minds. They expect large men in dirty clothes. One of them is thinking of drugs. Another sees motorcycles."

"Bella Vista does have a few bikers." Polly risked a glance behind them. A uniformed man had stepped into the alley, gun drawn. Polly whipped her head forward as she and Psyche turned the corner back onto the main road.

"Do not worry. He did not see us."

"Can we still risk Sun Valley? If the police are on alert, that could make things worse. Or maybe they're too busy now to be bothered by something else. I don't know. I'm not a criminal! What should we do?"

"I do not want to make your decision for you. But Polly, I will say that my next action should be to locate Nur-gahl. He will change form as soon as he is able. And it will be harder to detect him before he can kill again." Psyche stopped next to a parking meter and examined the dials with unmasked curiosity.

"Psyche, you promised to help Mom! Sun Valley is only two blocks east of here. One evening won't make a difference. Come with me, help Mom, then go chase that bear to the ends of the Earth." Polly tightened her grip on Psyche's sleeve.

"Your mom's life will not end tonight. Nur-gahl is clearly strong enough to kill already. Can you really justify the loss of a life, maybe several lives, because you have no patience left?" Psyche's voice was impossibly silky and calm.

"What about the silver inventory at Sun Valley? Caroline's uncle isn't going to do large silver orders anymore, remember? If we bail tonight and we don't get another chance soon, he'll use the raw materials and sell the finished products. We have no idea how long a large amount of this metal will be there!" Polly glared at Psyche who looked back with ancient fatigue. "I need you for the camera, the alarm, and any other electrical system I can't deal with." Polly stood rigid. Her fists were balled at her sides, knuckled white and bloodless.

"All right, Polly. Be aware that your soul may be stained tonight."

"Fine by me."

Polly marched the next two blocks to the jeweler's, doing her best to breathe deeply and reorient herself. She put her hand in her backpack and felt for the cotton drawstring bag that used to protect her mom's favorite purse. It was still there, empty and ready.

"This is it," said Polly, coming to an abrupt stop in front of a glass display window with bare white flocked pedestals.

"Are you sure Caroline is correct about the goods being present in this shop?" Psyche leaned toward the window, peering in until she was an inch from the glass.

"I think it's normal for shops to put their really valuable stuff in the safe overnight. Discourages good old-fashioned smash-and-grabs."

"Smash and . . . grabs?" Psyche paused and looked into Polly's mind. "Oh. Ah. All right. We will be more subtle than that."

"I hope so." Polly slipped into the small gap between Sun Valley's outer wall and the tax office next door. "Okay, now would be the time to do your electricity thingy."

"It would be wiser to enter the building and evaluate their wiring properly. You would not want me to destroy all power sources inside. That will inspire curiosity."

The stark gray door at the back of Sun Valley looked unassuming beside the empty patch of concrete—the size of roughly two parking spots—between the building and the alley. Polly could hardly hear Psyche's voice for the blood pumping between her ears. Every sound from the outside world was drowned out by her raspy breaths.

"Polly?" Psyche regarded her companion. "Do not be afraid. You must remain calm."

Polly's heart continued to thump in her chest. A siren sounded again, this time very far away.

"Sorry, I just . . ." Polly trailed off. They were about to commit a serious crime. Polly forced the image of her mom's face to her mind. She saw her wavy red-auburn hair, shining in the sun while they were on the beach. It wasn't enough. Polly forced to mind an image of her mom lying crumpled in a hospital bed. A family in the bed next to them joked and laughed behind a flimsy curtain; they were visiting a patient with a broken leg. They hadn't noticed the fragility of their neighbor and Polly didn't have the strength to reprimand them for being noisy while her mom tried to sleep. It was right after the start of treatment. Polly had been helpless then. But she wasn't helpless now, not with Psyche at her side.

"I'm good, Psyche. Let's do this." Polly met Psyche's gaze. In a blink she could tell that Psyche had pulled the images of her mom's treatment from her mind. *Good. I'm glad you saw.*

"Use your key. I will go inside and handle the electronics. You stay out here and watch for authorities."

The door opened with a soft click. Psyche slid inside the building and shut the door behind her. Polly scanned the street. She should have gone inside, too. What good was a lookout if the person inside had no idea what they were doing? Psyche might take forever trying to distinguish a security camera from an alarm system.

"Polly. I am finished. Come in." Psyche had opened the door without a sound, causing Polly to flinch at the sudden figure standing in front of her.

"Wow that was fast! I thought you'd need help." Polly followed Psyche inside the rear entrance to Sun Valley Jeweler's. Psyche lit their way with a gently crackling orb of white light in one palm.

"You forget, my friend, that I have ample information about your civilization, including technology and this region. I could not survive interdimensional travel and form-changing by any other means." Psyche led the way through a small storage room and into an office. "This is the room with the safe. One of the cameras is aimed at that door." She pointed at an obvious large metal door with a combination dial in the middle of it.

"Can you open it?" Polly's heart quickened again.

"I might pull the entire unit out of the wall."

"We knew there'd be a safe. But we also knew there would be no way to open it. I can't pick the lock—this isn't some spy movie. Maybe it is better if there's a show of force, at least in here. No one will think a couple of little girls tore open some kind of banker's vault." Polly cast her gaze up and around, despite knowing that Psyche had fried the security cameras.

Psyche inclined her head, ever so slightly, toward the safe. She gently lifted her free hand and concentrated, glaring hard at the wall. Her expression would have seemed spiteful under other circumstances. Polly didn't care. She felt hatred for that safe growing out of nowhere—it was all that stood between her and her mom's cure.

Metal creaked inside the strong box. Plaster around its frame popped and crumbled, but it remained in the wall. And then, very suddenly, the door popped open, revealing two large shelves. Psyche's orb of light illuminated velvet trays and flocked boxes on top. Bags and cardboard boxes filled the bottom layer.

Polly ripped open her backpack and stuffed in everything that looked like it contained metal. She filled her bag until she was sure she had a good deal more than a pound. Not all the contents would be pure silver, but there was no time to check. Then she slung the bag onto her back, grabbed Psyche's arm, and bolted out into the night.

"Psyche, we need to—"

A candy-sweet smell caught Polly just as she heard a faint hissing sound. She felt light-headed, and a second later her eyes rolled back in her head.

Polly woke up some time later on a bus bench next to the park downtown. Adrenaline kicked in—she snatched her backpack and launched herself onto the pavement. *What time is it? Where the hell is Psyche? Wait, the silver!* Polly flung the zipper open and rummaged in her bag. The haul was still intact.

She ran until she found her way back to the Rack Shack and the still-propped-open door in the rear. *Please, please, let something inside explain this!* She turned and took stock of the alley, praying for Psyche to appear. A blast of unforgiving wind answered instead.

Chapter 27

Polly leaned against the wall in the back hall of the Rack Shack, breathing slowly and deeply. She wanted to scream. After all the back-and-forth nonsense, she thought she'd convinced Psyche to leave Nur-gahl alone long enough to just heal her mom. *Why was that so hard? What did she do to me? Did she hear Nur-gahl somewhere nearby? Did she sense him hurting someone?*

Polly concentrated with an intensity only anger and grief could produce. She prayed Psyche could hear her thoughts. *Psyche, why? You could have given it one more night!* She tried with every fiber of her being to be understanding. She told herself Psyche wouldn't have slipped away without a good reason.

The plan discarded, Polly had to recalculate her next move. Chase Psyche? Get the silver home? Warn someone about Nur-gahl? Logic suggested that after the public vandalism of his escape and knowing that the entire town would be looking for a huge bear, Nur-gahl would choose a new form, something that would allow him to blend in with Bella Vista. Like a light switching on, she remembered her first priority—her alibi. She lurched off the wall and marched into the main room.

"Hey, ladies," she said as cheerfully as possible.

"Polly!" Brittany grinned.

"So how was . . . the bathroom?" Bethany's gaze drifted to the hallway that led out back. She leaned in and whispered, "You were gone a long time."

"It was . . . successful. Except that Psyche took off. She knocked me out somehow." Polly sat at their little bistro table and discreetly stuffed her backpack underneath. Caroline eyed the backpack with concern. Polly slid a key across the table. "I know you don't need this copy, but I thought you should have it anyway. You know, so you don't lose sleep."

"Thanks, Polly, that's thoughtful." Caroline gave a sympathetic smile.

Polly considered telling Caroline about the damage to the safe. *Nope, not right now*, she decided, her adrenaline receding.

"Forget the key! What about Psyche taking off? That big bag of 'product' is useless without her. What was she *thinking*?" Alya's whisper was laced with outrage.

Polly felt vindicated. "You're preaching to the choir. But there was a reason. We found the vet's office pretty much destroyed. It's obvious that something broke out." They leaned in closer. "I had a thought—and there isn't much we can do about it—but wouldn't it make sense for Nur-gahl to shift into something more inconspicuous after such a high-profile escape? The cops got there just as we left—we weren't seen. But if this demon-monster has half the wits she says he does, he'll know he can't go on as a bear."

"That does make sense. But if we don't know what we're looking for, or where, how do we find it? Him. Whatever." Alya gripped the table.

"On the plus side," said Caroline right as the music stopped. She quickly dropped to a whisper. "Whatever it changes into could be easier to fight."

"We should focus on the where for now. Alya, do you think we can get your dad's gun back?" Bethany stood and crossed her arms casually. Her calm demeanor gave Polly hope.

"I'm pretty sure he never missed it, so it should still be in our shed."

"So that just leaves the little problem of finding a couple of shape shifters hiding in the night." Brittany leaned against her pool cue again.

"We'll go back to the vet. I'll try to track it. Assuming Psyche can sense this thing on her own, wherever the creature went, we'll find her, too."

"Alya, you're my best friend!" Polly beamed at Alya.

"Hey!" Caroline looked offended. The rest of the girls shrugged their jackets back on.

"It's a figure of speech," Polly said, rolling her eyes.

The girls hung back from Lake Country Veterinary long enough to be sure that the caution tape roping off the property was the only remnant of the Bella Vista police.

"Great. It's worse than I thought. Every cop in town must have trampled across this porch." Alya kneeled down to examine the wood planks outside the entrance. The twins busied themselves worrying about the deep gouges left in the front door. Polly and Caroline watched the dark and motionless road.

"Is it a lost cause?" Polly finally asked after Alya spent way too long poking at muddy prints.

"Ummmmm . . . I don't think so." Alya wouldn't look up from the porch planks.

"Well, spit it out!" said Brittany.

"You said you thought he'd change, right?" Alya finally met Polly's wide eyes. She looked at Caroline and the twins, each leaning toward her. "I see a few smudged bear prints, and only on the top tier of the porch. That animal never went down the stairs." Alya took a deep breath. "But unless the officers walking around here were in bare feet, our demon bear turned into a human. A man, from the size of these prints." Alya lowered her flashlight, creating a crisp spotlight on a muddy footprint.

"So, you can track it?" said Bethany, pushing in front of her sister.

"It'll be less dangerous now, right? I mean, how much harm could single man cause," said Caroline.

"Let's go find out." Polly shifted her backpack. Alya lifted the shotgun from where she'd propped it against the porch railing. "If I don't lose his trail. Concrete doesn't exactly preserve footprints."

"Come on. Before it rains again," said Bethany as she hopped down the vet's front steps.

Polly and the girls marched down cold, dark streets, once familiar but now bristling with potential danger. Every time Alya rounded a corner, Polly's heart jumped into her throat. Every pause sent them into a silent, handwringing fit.

They finally stopped in front of a plain little rancher with a fruit tree out front. Polly looked over the simple yard—a few shrubs and shriveled flowerbeds quivered behind an unkempt lawn. The yard looked pitiful in the jaundiced glow of streetlights under a waning moon. Alya wore an uncertain frown on her face as she peered in through the side window of a beat-up camper van.

Polly couldn't take it any longer. "All right, what now?" She put her hands on her hips.

"Is he—it—in there?" Bethany pulled down her hood, joining Alya at the window.

"I don't think so." Alya strained and backed away, defeated. She circled around to the other side of the van. "Guys, come around here." She motioned to an open sliding door.

"Oh, great!" blurted Brittany.

"What?" snapped Polly.

"He must have stolen stuff out of the van. But he's long gone now." Bethany pushed her hair back. Polly angrily shoved her hands in her pockets. Alya sat down on the sidewalk.

"Okay then, where did he go?" Caroline peered into the van.

"We won't know now." Brittany kicked one of its tires.

"What do you mean? Alya, keep following whatever it was you were following," said Caroline.

"She can't. She was following bare footprints, or at least whatever fragments she could find. Now the thing is wearing sneakers. Like the thousands of other people walking around Bella Vista. We're done."

Polly looked around for some sign of what to do next. "AAAAAAAHHHHH!" she shouted and punched the van's sliding door. Her strength surprised her, but so did the pain. She shook her hand in the air.

"I'm so sorry, Polly." Alya rubbed the back of her neck and dropped her head to her knees.

"You have nothing to be sorry for. Are you sure you can't pick up anything from here? Look inside the van, maybe there's a shoe print you could follow or something?" Polly paced on the sidewalk behind Alya and the twins.

"I'll try, but it would take a miracle. Even my dad would have trouble with this. He's awesome and all, but—" Alya broke off as a loud *CRACK-ACK-ACK* exploded in the air behind them.

Each girl turned to see the source of the noise. A blue arc of electricity shot into the air and died. Then another.

Chapter 28

Sy'kai, where are you, whelp? I am ready to end your existence now. Come and meet your death.

Psyche followed Polly away from Sun Valley Jeweler's at a brisk jog.

Actually . . . perhaps I should feed for a time before I find you. Watching your conscience torture you will be much more entertaining. I can see your plan for these useless human children. Oh, all the death I shall lay at your feet—so much fresh blood on your hands.

Polly slowed to a walk, head down. Psyche stopped mid-stride.

You DO care for this creature. That settles it; my first stop is your pet's mother. After that, perhaps we can find a way to show your little girl exactly who you really are. She thinks of you as a hero. We know the truth though.

Psyche took one heartbeat to decide.

Your depravity knows no bounds, brother. So be it. I will meet your challenge.

Psyche sensed Nur-gahl's location. He was close. She caught up to Polly, silently stretched out her hand, and released a cloud of gas. Polly's body went slack and Psyche caught her. A nearby bench on a field of grass would have to do. Psyche deposited Polly there.

She took off then at a sprint, hurrying toward Nur-gahl. As she ran, she tried to sense his form. She was definitely not running toward a large snarling bear—that much she knew. Hot tingles raced across her skin as she crossed the overgrown lawn of a dark, dilapidated house. She stopped in her tracks again as Polly's friend Nick exited through the front door.

"Nur-gahl?" Psyche frowned as she processed the combination of her enemy's thoughts and the visual input of Polly's crush.

"No, Nick." Nur-gahl's mouth crept into a disturbing crescent—a total failure of a smile.

"What purpose does this serve? Why play this game?" Psyche concentrated, extending her awareness in a sphere that engulfed the surrounding run-down homes and the rest of the street. Mercifully, only a few minds slept in the houses farther down.

Nur-gahl slowly descended a set of concrete steps that stank of mildew. Psyche felt his disgust—at the home, at the town. But most of all, with her.

"Creating fresh opportunities for your suffering is the only satisfaction I have left. If you were not such a liability, I would keep you alive simply to torment you." Nur-gahl stood a breath from Psyche's face. His replication of Nick's features had turned out perfectly. Psyche's stomach clenched.

"I have regained my memories. I understand your anger. We will agree to disagree on the necessity of my actions at the Temple."

"Your justification for killing our people—our MOTHER—are of no interest to me. They never were. It was unforgivable then. Nothing has changed." Fake-Nick looked away. Nur-gahl's telekinetic power knocked Psyche backwards. She hit the ground with a *smack*. He strode toward her casually.

"I do still want your gifts, though, sister. I have spent so much time dreaming of the worlds I will visit and the havoc I will unleash once I am able to manipulate energy and space." Nur-gahl kneeled next to Psyche's face as she gasped to regain her breath. "Most of all, I know your essence will be delicious." He laced his fingers into her long blonde hair, cupping her scalp. He closed his fist and pulled upward as Psyche cried out.

Nur-gahl brushed Psyche's cheek with his free hand. Then he gripped her jaw and began to suck the life force from her. White light illuminated their faces, catching both sets of blue eyes with an eerie glow as one soul consumed the other. With great effort, Psyche raised her hand to summon energy as she fought to close her mouth.

She fired a bolt of electricity through Nur-gahl's chest, forcing him back. Psyche clamped her mouth shut, wrenching her head to the side to break their connection.

"You brat!" Nur-gahl snarled and forced himself to stand. He punched Psyche in the face with all his strength. A loud *SLAP* sent her to the ground. Nur-gahl collapsed next to her as they both struggled to compose themselves.

Nur-gahl extended his arm to a window across the street. Weakened, he drew only a fragment of energy from whatever was there on the other side of the glass. But it was enough. Nur-gahl rose and slung Psyche over his shoulder as she lost consciousness.

Psyche woke tied to a wood chair in the middle of a dark, bare room. Trash littered the floor. She tried to cry out. A sour rag had been shoved in her mouth and tied on with the same fabric that restrained her wrists and ankles

"Mmmmmmm. MMMMMMMM!" Psyche sucked air in through her nose, forcing the loudest sound she could manage from behind the wad of cloth.

"I am delighted that you had a chance to rest. We have so much work to do tonight." The strangeness of Nick's voice caught Psyche off guard, then she remembered she was actually hearing Nur-gahl. She whipped her head back and forth, trying to pick him out of the shadows.

"MMMMMMMM!" Psyche's stifled attempt at yelling drained her courage.

"I truly am enjoying this body! I see why you like humans so much. I should have tried one myself much earlier. Far less power than my first shape, but the sensations are thrilling. The ideas! I cannot thank you enough for drawing out our stay in this world. But I have forgotten my manners." Nur-gahl stepped into a shaft of moonlight. He reached around Psyche's head and untied her gag.

"HELP! HELP M—" A strong backhand knocked the words from her mouth.

"If you plan to carry on with that rather fruitless noise, I can certainly put this piece of cloth back in your mouth. It would give us the ongoing privacy we would need to allow me to experiment with how best to inflict pain, but not death, on a human body." Nur-gahl's cold voice trembled with a world's worth of hate.

Psyche took a long centering breath and held it deep within her core. She shrugged off her anxiety and the fear she felt pulsing through her veins. Every day in this form had made her more human, and right now, she needed her morphling strength of mind.

"You were right, this world has softened me." Psyche's eyes seized on a flash on the floor, mostly concealed by a crumpled paper. "Perhaps my time is finally over as a result." Then she propelled herself in the direction of the concealed flash. She landed face first, but sucked as hard as she could until she managed to inhale a piece of copper pipe. A surge of vigor flowed through her, tingling in her arms and legs, allowing her to rip through her fabric bonds. The chair broke as she fought. She remembered her time as a winged serpent and the strength of those muscles. And then the sheer power of her legs as a horned horse. She still, as a human, had access to so much energy.

"Or *I* could kill *you* instead!" And she let loose a crackling bolt of blue from each hand.

Electricity engulfed Nur-gahl, causing his entire body to shake, filling the grimy house with the smell of burnt flesh. He struggled hard, fighting to keep the cells of his body from exploding. Psyche shut off her power, panting from exertion. Nur-gahl collapsed in a heap.

"Bitch!" he snapped as he rolled over.

"Silence, monster! Leave this world with me now, for your own good. I will take you someplace where you can be at peace."

"I want to go HOME! Take me to the Astral Temple!"

"Never. You will never return to the Temple, not if I can help it."

"Then you leave me no choice." Nur-gahl focused his telekinetic power on Psyche as she let loose another massive arc of electricity. The charge sliced a hole through the roof and Psyche was heaved off the ground. She screamed. Beams of wood rained down upon her, but she blocked them from striking her head.

Psyche's fear switched back to rage and she unleashed another intense bolt, fighting to aim it while Nur-gahl flung her body back and forth inside the fragile building. He flipped her like a rag doll until the back of her head cracked against a truss beam. Psyche fell limp in the air.

Chapter 29

Polly's feet pounded the road as she hurtled toward the telltale blue electricity in the sky. She heard the clomping of her friends' shoes on the dusty asphalt behind her. The blue light went out.

Polly rounded a corner and stopped to scan the street, frantically searching for something specific. She needed more information. The girls caught up to her, panting. They heard another female scream from an abandoned house nearby and a male voice barking back in response. Polly took off, crossed the yard, and burst through the door.

Inside, she found Psyche bound with zip-ties on the floor as Nick looked on.

"Polly, run!" Psyche shouted as she twisted her body to unleash a bolt at Nick. His face contorted with pain as the charge knocked him into a wall. A stray arc of energy shot up out of a fresh hole in the ceiling.

"Psyche, what the hell!" Polly yelled.

"You have to get out of here, all of you!" Psyche used her telekinesis to keep Polly from getting closer.

"Polly, please help me." Nick's voice was weak. He forced himself to sit up. "This girl is crazy. We have to stop her." He sat against the wall, coughing, clutching pieces of torn fabric stretched across his ribs.

"Psyche, this is Nick! He's our friend!" Polly shouted.

"What happened here? Psyche, you need to explain yourself," Alya said, pointing her dad's shotgun at Psyche.

"Girls, you are mistaken. This is not your friend." Psyche wrestled against the bonds on her arms and legs. "Would I be tied up if this was your Nick?"

"Alya, put the gun down, she could be right." Bethany extended her arm toward Alya.

"But what if she's lying? Maybe she's changed her mind about helping Polly's mom. Maybe she'd rather just cut and run back to god only knows where! Remember the bear? You could tell it wasn't normal. This is definitely Nick!" Alya's chest rose and fell rapidly.

"Listen to Alya. I'm here to help. I found her like this. I have no idea who tied her up." Nick's voice was thick with empathy. He looked from Polly to Alya with earnest concern.

Polly was torn. He sounded so much like the caring, gentle guy she'd fallen for back in the eighth grade.

"Let's just take a moment to think here," Brittany said, trying to sound commanding.

"We should at least cut the zip ties. Haven't we been trying to help Psyche all along?" Caroline pleaded.

"Untie her and she is bound to really do some damage," said Nick.

"We have every reason to trust Psyche," said Bethany.

"And we shouldn't trust Nick?" Alya's tone was incredulous. Her arms quivered as she held the gun trained on Psyche's chest.

"Nick," said Polly, trying to catch his gaze. "How did you know Psyche was in here?"

"I heard a scream."

"I screamed because this is Nur-gahl and he attacked me! He brought me here so he could absorb my essence and start ravaging your world!" shouted Psyche. She struggled harder and an arc of blue energy shot from her hands across the room.

Alya fired, sending a spray of buckshot at the slim girl. Psyche cried in pain as the shot ripped into her chest, and she crumpled like a wilted flower. Instinctively, Alya reloaded the shotgun.

All the girls screamed.

"Excellent, truly," Nick said. "Nice work. I am in your debt." He dusted himself off and got to his feet.

"What?" Polly rounded at Nick, rage in her eyes.

Alya whirled the shotgun around at Nick. "Don't move!"

"You know that will not kill me. I will only be angrier the next time we meet." Nick grinned maliciously as he backed toward the door. Alya's arms shook as she fought to keep her gun held high, pointed straight at Nick's chest. He gave an arrogant wave and jogged off into the night. Alya's arms collapsed. Polly ran to the door and watched Nick disappear around the corner.

"Psyche, are you awake?" Brittany was at Psyche's side with two fingers on the unconscious girl's neck.

"Copper. We need to find some copper, fast." Bethany slid down next to Brittany as Polly, shocked, followed to where Psyche lay limp on the floor.

Caroline searched Alya's bag and handed a pocket knife to Brittany who in turn sawed at the bonds on Psyche's wrists. The plastic popped open and Brittany moved on to the ankles.

"Check the walls," blurted Caroline. "Old pipes are usually made of copper."

Alya snapped out of her daze. "Oh god, what have I done?"

"That thing knew the shotgun wouldn't kill him," Caroline said, searching the far corner and adjacent wall, "so it won't kill Psyche either. She needs a boost, that's all."

"He looked and sounded exactly like Nick. I wasn't one hundred percent sure myself until afterwards," said Polly. She shot Alya a reassuring look.

"I should have listened to her. I should have believed her." Alya's voice quivered as she picked through the garbage at her feet.

"Psyche knew we were confused. She can hear our thoughts. I'm sure she understands," Bethany said as she plucked a pellet from Psyche's arm.

"I found some pipe. I think its copper. Can someone help me?" Caroline tugged uselessly on a piece of pipe exposed by demolished drywall.

Alya rushed to grab the section of pipe above Caroline's hands. "At least this happened in an abandoned house. No change jars or jewelry boxes to raid, but rip the plumbing out and nobody cares." They pulled in unison and the pipe groaned and creaked. With a loud crack the girls went stumbling backwards.

"Will this be enough?" Brittany asked, accepting the three-foot-long section of pipe from Alya and Caroline.

"I found these on the floor, too." Caroline handed some loose pipe cuttings to Bethany.

"Start with the smaller ones," said Brittany.

Bethany lifted a candy-sized pipe piece to Psyche's mouth. She waved it under the delicate porcelain nose. Blood ran down either cheek, dark as molasses in the low light. Psyche did not move. Bethany carefully opened Psyche's mouth and put the tube inside.

Psyche twitched. Blue light escaped her lips as she started chewing on the metal.

"Thank you, thank you, thank you." Alya put her face in her hands and sighed.

Bethany continued to feed the other odd bits to Psyche, who ate in her sleep.

"How should I . . .?" Brittany held the last and longest section of pipe in front of Psyche. The alien girl sat up—her eyes snapped open. She jumped to her feet and grabbed the pipe. Psyche ate hungrily, like a child with an oversized stick of licorice. The pipe released high-pitch squeaks while she tore through it as smoothly as an industrial machine. Neither her jaw nor her shining white teeth ever hinted at resistance from the thick metal. The humans in the room stared in awe.

Psyche paused a moment after she finished, looking as though she might vomit. She closed her eyes, opened her mouth, and let out a sound that rang like a singing bowl. A glow like a television screen in the dark lit the girls' faces—they watched Psyche with fascination. The ringing sound stopped and Psyche spat several shotgun pellets from her mouth. More pellets rained from her clothes.

"Please, do not shoot me ever again. That was unpleasant." Psyche rubbed the side of her jaw that had hit the ground. No marks remained on her skin, but Psyche seemed rattled.

"I'm so sorry. I'm so, so very sorry." Alya's words tumbled out, overflowing with sincerity.

"I know you believed Nur-gahl's disguise. You all did. Well, most of you." Psyche smiled at Bethany.

"I guess I have a little psychic twinkle, too." Bethany gave a thin smile.

"No, you do not." Psyche's matter-of-fact tone and easy smile made the girls laugh.

"She's finally got a sense of humor." Polly clapped Psyche on the back.

"Um, has everyone forgotten that we should probably go find Nick? The fake one, I mean. Like now," Caroline said, peeking nervously out the front door.

"Give me a moment." Psyche closed her eyes, breathing in and out, in and out. "Get a map. I know where he has gone."

"Topographic or street?" asked Alya.

"The one you are picturing with 'pink roads' all over."

Alya paused. "I think that's officially the first time I've had my mind read. Anyway, it's a tourist map of Greater Berktonas Valley. They sell it at gas stations." She dug in her bag and handed Psyche a folded rectangle.

"We should go out into the light." Psyche led them all outside and to the streetlight next to the camper van, the door of which was still wide open.

"This place," she said, pointing to the map. "A house. Nur-gahl is inside already, waiting for me. He stole a vehicle. He knows your security people are still searching for a dangerous bear. In fact, they are quite worried; all their attention is on the matter. As for Nur-gahl, try not to think of him—or me—until we arrive. We cannot surprise him any longer, just as you cannot surprise me. We will have to make do by shielding as much as we can. And do not call him by your friend's name. He will use that against you. Nur-gahl chose to become a replica of Nick after reading Polly's mind. He knew it was his best chance of manipulating her. He also probed Nick's mind to achieve such a believable copy."

"This just keeps getting better." Brittany gritted her teeth. Polly had never seen the twin so angry.

"You pointed at a remote road on the other side of Crescent Lake," Bethany said. "We can't walk there. And we don't have our bikes."

"It's way too cold. I'm not biking," said Caroline flatly.

"Ditto. Let's wait until morning." Alya flipped her hood up.

"We would do well got go now. But I should not make a portal; I will need all my energy to fight Nur-gahl. We will take a vehicle of our own. This one. And quickly. The owner will not miss it as he is away on a trip. But there is a man in that house"—Psyche pointed at a reasonably well-maintained character home down the road—"who plans to come check on this property soon, as a favor to the man who is gone."

"So . . . we're about to have company?" Polly craned around the van, surveying the other side of the street.

"Next to a clearly broken-into van?" Brittany moved to guard the door.

"Who's going to drive?" Polly climbed into the vehicle. She tidied up some magazines and dirty laundry strewn across the bench seats and tossed it all into the back. The other girls piled in.

"My mom has taken me out driving a couple of times," Alya said with some uncertainty. "I could do it. There isn't much traffic anyway."

"I'm not allowed to even *touch* a wheel until I'm sixteen," Caroline said.

"I will operate the vehicle." Psyche climbed into the driver's seat and pressed her palm with her thumb and forefinger. Polly noticed a subtle blue glow through Psyche's eyelids and mouth. "There, I've learned to drive."

"This is gonna end badly," said Alya.

"She'll be fine," Bethany said as she shut the van door.

Caroline tried her best to look comfortable while perched on the edge of her seat, desperately not wanting to make contact with anything inside the van. Psyche touched her finger to the ignition. Polly saw a tiny spark shoot from the girl's fingertip and enter the key slot. The engine roared to life.

"What about the guy in the house down the street?" Polly whispered.

"He is busy putting on a pair of shoes, but one of them has a knot in the laces that is giving him quite a bit of trouble."

"Then let's get moving!" Brittany gripped a handle on the panel behind the driver's seat.

"All right." Psyche had to stretch her leg to engage the clutch, but she got the van into drive and lurched out onto the road.

"I thought you said you could drive!" cried Alya as Caroline clung to her arm.

"I learned the motions and laws of driving. My practical skill level will improve." Psyche looked into the rear-view mirror and grinned at the girls in the back. She reached a stop sign and turned to Polly, smiling more broadly as she flicked the turn signal.

"Pride looks weird on you, Psyche. Just watch the road. Please." Polly braced herself with both hands on the dashboard as Psyche took the corner a bit too wide.

Psyche's eyes fluttered then. She rested her forehead on the steering wheel for a moment before snapping back. She concentrated on the road ahead, leaning toward the wheel—overly large in her delicate hands.

Consciousness left her suddenly and her forehead hit the wheel.

Chapter 30

"Psyche!" Polly shouted. She grabbed the wheel to keep them on the road.

"Sorry!" Psyche came to, her fingers fumbling around the wheel while she strained to re-orient herself.

"Okay, pull over. There's a park up ahead. We might look a bit creepy hanging out in a parked camper van, but it's better than you crashing us into a telephone pole." Polly pointed at a parking lot. Psyche turned in and parked.

"Well . . . that was interesting," Brittany said.

"She obviously needs more time to recover." Bethany glared at her sister.

"How long do you need, Psyche? We don't want to rush you," Alya said, looking to Polly for encouragement. Polly shrugged.

"I do not need a great deal of time, but you are correct, I still require rest." Psyche nestled back into the driver's seat and closed her eyes.

"Should we be worried about the police looking for this van?" Caroline leaned forward, barely touching her seat.

"Try the radio," Brittany said. "Maybe there's something about the incident at the vet." She sounded eager to hear something scandalous.

"I'd settle for a good song. We need the distraction," Polly said. She turned on the radio and fiddled with the dial to find her favorite station, 101.5 Star FM.

"And welcome to another Power Hour with Jerr the Bear at the Valley's only home for Rock and Roll," a man crooned. "Here to kick off what I can only describe as the strangest evening of all time here in quiet little Bella Vista, this is Blondie's 'Rapture.'"

"What do you think he meant by that?" Bethany asked. The girls looked at each other as Debbie Harry's melodic voice rang through the vehicle.

"Change it to the news," said Caroline, calm as she could manage through her frayed nerves.

"I can't handle news right now," Alya said, exhausted.

Do they know about you in town? Or is it just the escaped bear? Polly thought at Psyche. A sudden stab of fear ripped through her gut. She felt for the backpack under her seat. "Oh my god," she said aloud, "maybe he means Sun Valley on top of the bear escape. Or the damage to that abandoned house?"

"This isn't turning into much of a distraction," said Alya as the song shifted into a catchy rap.

"No authorities in town are looking for any of you. Your parents are all contentedly watching television believing that you are at each other's houses as you said you would be." Psyche spoke softly, eyes shut.

"Are you sure? You really saw into the minds of all our parents?" Caroline wanted to believe Psyche, but the biology honor student in her wanted empirical evidence. Polly clicked the radio off.

"Caroline, your disbelief in my abilities and the nature of my species is understandable, but I do not know how to convince you, beyond what you have already seen." Psyche opened her weary eyes; they glowed in the moonlight.

"I believe you. So do the others. Mostly," said Polly.

"Tell us more about where you're from." Bethany shifted in her seat, inching closer.

"My home? Ask Polly. She has seen it."

"What!" the others belted in unison.

"It was kind of like a vision. A shared dream." Polly heard the tension in her voice and felt heat bloom in her cheeks. "Psyche is from somewhere inside a nebula. It doesn't make sense, but I can't explain it any other way. She called it the Astral Temple. It was soft but made of stone. And surrounded by stars. And space. I felt like I was in the middle of the universe, but then we were suddenly in a meadow. It was like a strange trip—stranger than any drug. I think. I don't actually know from experience, of course."

"Why did you leave your home?" Brittany asked Psyche. "You haven't said much about it except that there was some kind of conflict. Did this demon guy chase you out?"

"Brittany!" Bethany reprimanded her sister. Polly felt the urge to do similarly, but she wanted to hear Psyche's answers even more.

"In a manner of speaking, yes, I was chased out. I had to destroy what you would call my mother. She was the oldest of my kind and the creator of our Temple. I do not know why she became the creature she did. For eons, she was a beacon of peace and serenity. One day she discovered a race of brilliantly creative creatures living on a rock orbiting a star, much like your people, your planet, and your sun." Psyche paused and the girls crowded in closer.

"Curiosity drove my mother to leave the Temple and cross into that mortal world. Gathering information for our archives was typically a task for younger morphlings. Nevertheless, she shifted into a body and explored not just the planet but also what it was like to be of that species. I am not sure how it happened, but she accidentally consumed one of the beings in that world. The sensation drove her mad with desire. She began to feed, off emotion and flesh alike. In time, she gathered others of my kind and brought them on raiding parties. After ravaging that first world, they moved on to another, and another. They used our own archives to select the best worlds to consume. I refused to participate, as did some of my sisters and brothers at first. One by one, though, they all eventually joined her. One day, when I was alone in the Temple, I devised a plan. My gift of manipulating spacetime allowed me to seal off our Temple. I had honed this gift, thinking I might one day need to protect my people from something, though I was not sure what. I waited until I sensed my mother and the others returning from their first visit to a new world. They were drunk on the rush of feeding for the first time in many years. I waited for them to be traveling between the world they had left and the safety of our home and sealed off the Temple at the exact moment a fissure in existence would crush any stationary particles. They all died. All except one of my brothers who had managed to slip into the Temple before my seal was complete."

"Nur-gahl," Polly said somberly.

"He really does hate you." Bethany's voice was equally empathetic.

"And probably all of us now," said Alya.

"Yes, he hates most everything living. He reviles anything mortal. It is how he justifies feeding. His essence cannot be saved." Psyche sat up straight and restarted the van. "All right. It is time to finish this war forever."

Chapter 31

The trip to Lakeshore Drive was jerky and slow. Polly noticed that it had been several minutes since they'd seen another car. She looked at her watch—it was ten o'clock. Late enough for the town to be in bed, and for her mom to start worrying. Polly prayed that her mom had fallen asleep in front of the television, cuddled up in a blanket and not missing her daughter. She would have been watching *The Tonight Show*, although she frequently complained that it was time for Johnny Carson to retire. Without Polly to nudge her off to bed, her mom would sleep on the couch until she woke up in the wee hours of the morning, stiff and uncomfortable. Polly could still make it home in time to help her to bed without her being any the wiser about the robbery at Sun Valley, an undead bear rampage at a vet's office, or a supernatural battle by the lake. Her mom might give her a hard time for staying up too late, but only if she caught sight of the clock on her way to bed.

Psyche hit the brakes hard at a stop sign, yanking Polly from her thoughts.

"We should've started with a smaller vehicle for your first drive." Polly smiled at Psyche, who kept her eyes on the road.

Polly went back to looking out the windshield, picturing the sort of waterfront home they would find on the notoriously wealthy Lakeshore Drive; it would be new and clean, hardly lived in and full of designer furnishings. It wasn't a bad choice for a place to hide out—much more comfortable and classier than the slated-for-demolition heap they'd just left. Would it be a good place to fight a non-corporeal demon? Was there such a place? She pushed aside the tingling dread creeping up the back of her neck.

Lakeshore Drive had clean, fresh pavement and manicured lawns. Under the bright streetlights, the neighborhood looked almost plastic. Psyche slowed the van to a crawl until they reached an elegant, if impractically large, home with two-story glass windows that wrapped around from the living room to the balcony overlooking the lake. Polly decided immediately that no full-time resident of Bella Vista could afford such a property. Psyche stopped at the edge of a gated driveway and put the van in park.

"Hey, this is pretty swanky. If your shapeshifter boy isn't here, I say we pop in for a visit anyway," Brittany said, poking her face between Psyche and Polly.

"Are you sure this is the right place? Why would this monster come all the way out to a glass palace to fight you?" Bethany asked.

"The construction and design of this home, with so many windows, reminds Nur-gahl of the Astral Temple. I think even if the owner had been here, Nur-gahl would have killed him and taken the building." Psyche turned to assess Polly and the others.

BANG! BA-BANG! BANG! Explosions rocked the van from underneath.

"Holy shit, what was that!" shouted Polly as the van settled again.

"I'd say we just blew all four tires for no reason. Nothing freaky about that," Alya said sarcastically as she forced open the van's sliding door.

"Be careful!" cried Caroline.

Bethany and Brittany hopped out behind Alya, followed by Polly and Psyche. Caroline joined them a moment later as a bright yellow light flicked on inside the house.

"Looks like someone's home after all," Polly said, spotting a silhouette in the window. Nick, or Nur-gahl pretending to be Nick, smiled back at her. For the first time in her life, she wanted to be as far from that face as possible.

"Be sure you have both the pellet and rock salt shotgun shells at the ready," Psyche said to Alya. "We will stick with our original plan. You open a wound and enflame it with salt so that I can destroy his body and seal him in a portal."

She did not break eye contact with Nur-gahl as she spoke.

"Couldn't we get him to change into something else first? So it doesn't feel like we're killing Nick?" Polly wanted to look away, but she was afraid of giving Nur-gahl any advantage. Instinct told her not to turn her back on a predator.

"Nur-gahl knows that using Nick's form makes you all uncomfortable. A bear, you were willing to fight and kill. The face of a friend, one you have strong affection for, is amusing for him. Nur-gahl will not relinquish the form so long as he is having fun." Psyche turned to Alya. "Are you ready?"

"Ready as I'll ever be." Alya opened, checked, and snapped her shotgun shut before patting her jacket pocket for the extra shells.

"I want the twins to remain in the van," said Psyche. "If any of you require medical attention after this fight, and if I am dead, you will need them."

"Bethany can stay, but I'm coming. You guys need all the help you can get." Brittany stepped forward, glaring at Nur-gahl.

"There's no way I'm staying out here alone," Bethany said firmly.

"Keep your cool, ladies." Polly followed Psyche to the front door, her every step pulsing with terror. She spotted the barrel of Alya's gun in her peripheral vision but kept contact with the demon wearing her crush's face. A numbing chill came over her body. *He's just a copy. That's not really Nick.* She repeated the thought to herself like a mantra.

"Stay close to me. Nur-gahl wants to separate us. He wants to frighten and consume you, one by one. Do not be fooled by any illusions," Psyche said, and entered through the front door.

"Wait, illusions?" Caroline said with a hint of panic. Polly took her hand and squeezed.

Alya shifted her aim from the bay window to the front door.

"Welcome, friends of Sy'kai." Nick's voice echoed through the entryway.

"Do not answer him," Psyche instructed the group.

"I don't think I'd know what to say." Brittany risked a quick peek around Psyche's shoulder.

"Where is he?" Bethany said.

"He has to be in there. He's playing with us," Polly said, still holding

Caroline's hand. Neither wanted to let go. Brittany grabbed Polly's other hand.

"When you get a shot, take it," Psyche said to Alya.

"Done." Alya followed Psyche carefully.

Polly smelled iron in the air as they crossed the threshold. A vaulted ceiling soared overhead. They rounded a corner into the next room and saw Nurgahl-as-Nick resting casually against the head of a long gleaming black dining table. His arms were crossed. He wore crisp jeans and a collared white shirt, appearing older and more sophisticated than the real Nick.

And with a quick flick of his wrist he sent Psyche flying sideways. Alya froze in shock. A flick of his other hand and she, too, was knocked onto her back.

"Now then, girls, who would like to take a walk with me?"

Chapter 32

Polly's apprehension melted away under Nick's warm gaze. *It's not really Nick.* Polly's inner voice coached her. *This is Nur-gahl, don't let him trick you!*

"Of course, I am your friend. I would like to be more than that, if you would only let me. I know you want the same thing. I am not trying to trick you; all of you can trust me." Nur-gahl's smile tormented Polly. Nick had never looked at her this way, no matter how hard she'd wished for it. She took a deep breath, balling her fists so that her fingernails dug into her palms.

"Polly, there is no reason for anything bad to happen here tonight. If you and your friends turn Sy'kai over to me, all your troubles will be over, just like that." Nur-gahl snapped with Nick's right hand.

Polly took another deep breath.

"Polly, don't listen to—" Brittany was cut off suddenly. "AHHHH! Get them off! GET THEM OFF ME!" She clawed and scraped at her arms and torso. Polly looked and saw nothing on her friend but her clothes.

"Polly. Don't move," Caroline whispered in her ear.

"What do you mean? There's nothing there." Polly glanced at Caroline, following her gaze down an empty hallway.

"They're coming from that room!" Brittany shrieked again, still trying to pick invisible creatures off her body.

"We have to get out of here!" Bethany squealed.

"Polly! Look! It's so huge. Those teeth! Psyche, wake up. HELP US!" Caroline cried.

Polly sized up Caroline and the twins, all lost in their own hallucinations. Alya and Psyche remained unconscious on the ground. Brittany snapped and ran outside. Moments later, Caroline and Bethany did the same.

An elaborate crystal chandelier hovered overhead, casting warm yellow light around the room. The hardwood floor gleamed, reminding Polly of the Astral Temple.

"You have seen my home. No mortal creature has—you should feel privileged. Do you understand why I have to go back?" Nur-gahl's imitation of Nick's voice was now perfect. The plea in his tone tugged at Polly's heart. "Sy'kai will leave you as soon as she heals your mother. You know that, correct? That is, if she performs the healing at all. You already doubt her intent to keep her promise. *I* would stay with you. *I* would be everything you want."

The words struck Polly as inauthentic, but he *sounded* so much like Nick. She tried to concentrate on all the ways in which Nur-gahl was *not* Nick, to remind herself. *No, wait, he's reading your mind. Don't give him any more ammunition,* she thought, chastising her own brain.

The boy Polly had spent the last year trying not to love took a step closer. His steel eyes locked with hers. She tried to step back but physically couldn't move.

"Do you want to leave?" he sneered. "I think not."

Nur-gahl was mere inches from Polly's face when he lifted his hand and touched her cheek. Polly couldn't look away; the warm palm tenderly cradling her jaw felt alive with passion. Her heart pounded.

Nick leaned forward. "If I kill Sy'kai, I will have her powers. That is how it works with our kind." Warm breath kissed Polly's ear. She felt her pulse beating in her eardrums. "I could heal your mother. I could take us to the real Temple, and we could come back to Earth as often as we like. We could be happy wherever we wanted to be, live, go, explore. I would show you endless facets of the universe."

"You don't want me. You can't take me through a portal. And you certainly don't want to help anyone here. You're playing with your next meal. You can't fool me," Polly said, doing her best to muster conviction. A wave of frustration crashed over her, washing away her fear and reluctance. Polly wanted this private war to end, one way or another, tonight. Anger throbbed inside her chest. *How dare he manipulate me like this! I'm done being afraid of this evil monster!*

"I have already won. I can feel how much your body wants this one. Does it matter that the mind inside is different? I would go as far as to say better, too. And you are wrong; I do want a companion. Your Nick does not want you. He has no interest in you whatsoever, I promise. I, on the other hand, want everything about you. And that excites you. Do not lie to me." Nur-gahl's imitation of Nick's soothing voice faltered as his frustration surfaced.

Polly cracked a small smile. "You can fool my body. Maybe you can trick my mind, too, if we stand here long enough. I could do the same thing to a dog. That wouldn't make me impressive—it would make me horrible. And I believe everything Psyche told me, about you and her home. I think you're an abomination. Wear the skin of the boy I like. Dangle my mom's life over my head. It doesn't make you special or important. You're a monster, whether you look like one or not," she finished, feeling fresh rage swirling around her.

Nur-gahl backed away from Polly and winked at her. He paused, then lurched at her, but instead of striking, he reached behind the spot where she stood anchored in front of a fireplace. He pulled a sculpture off the mantle—a wood carving of a pair of dolphins spiraled around waves.

"You think Psyche told you everything about us? I doubt she even bothered to try. Your kind could have no meaningful conception of what it is like to exist outside of a prison of flesh. Morphlings were eternal. We were made to become, end, transform, and begin again." Nur-gahl moved his hands around the sculpture and the dolphins began to dance. "The loss of my kind was more tragic than any genocide your world has seen. We were … pure magic."

Polly watched the wood dolphins slide gracefully up and around. The fine lines in the grain of their bodies moved—it was lifelike, as if they'd become real. Nur-gahl set the sculpture on the table and pulled his hands back. The wood waves slid onto the glass surface and the dolphins began to jump and play, in and out of the glass like it was water. The table and sculpture blended together, a surreal stage. The dolphins released tiny chirps and the water splashed. Utter delight filled Polly. She let herself fall into a trance, briefly forgetting about Psyche, her friends—even her mom.

One of the wood dolphins turned to look at Polly, then the other. Frowns appeared on their little faces and they swam toward her, jumping and diving as they moved. Together, the creatures reached the thick black metal frame at the edge of the table. Their faces warped, becoming elongated muzzles. Their smooth skin flaked off in rough layers. Their playful eyes, once sparkling, went black and radiated malice.

The dolphins were no longer dolphins; they were aggressive lizards with giant beak-tipped mouths. They crawled up and out of the table-sea and grew as if it fed them, making them larger with every wave. Their shining, scaly skin reflected the tiny beams from the chandelier. They perched on the table's edge, opening large mouths packed with glass teeth. Their jaws unzipped outward, doubling the volume of fangs, all of them aimed at Polly. Each let out a screech.

They leapt toward her, zealous and hungry, clawed feet ready to rend the muscles from her bones.

Chapter 33

Before the wood-glass lizards could strike, wires of prickly blue light passed an inch from Polly's eyes and fried them in mid-air. Their charred figures fell, breaking into pieces as they hit the hardwood.

"Theatrics were always your strength, brother." Psyche appeared beside Polly.

"And choosing a moment was yours, sister." Nur-gahl concentrated his telekinetic energy at Psyche, lifting her off the ground. "A minute later and I would be enjoying quite a show. I had planned to have those creations feed me pieces of your new pet. It would have been delicious to feel her fear in the air and taste her blood on this sensitive mortal tongue. You cost me a lovely feast." Nur-gahl turned Psyche over in the air, toying with her.

Psyche fought back, but Nur-gahl held her aloft.

This is hopeless, Polly thought, watching helplessly. *He's stronger than her. There's nothing we can do. Hate really is stronger than love.*

"You humans are such simple wretches," said Nur-gahl, looking to Polly with disdain.

Alya finally lifted her head and pushed herself up. Nur-gahl either didn't notice or didn't care—his eyes stayed locked on Polly.

"I am disappointed in the meal you will now make, little girl. Then again, once I rid myself of my sister and this entourage of hers, I will be free to find the best of your kind. Perhaps I will make some new creatures and let them shred my prey into pieces, giving me satisfaction after all."

Two things happened at once: A fresh jolt of electricity hit Nur-gahl in the head right as a shotgun blast tore into his chest. His body flew back into the wall. Alya kept her firearm pointed at Nur-gahl's collapsed figure as Psyche guided herself back down to the ground.

"Fire again when he stands," Psyche said, moving to stand beside Alya.

Hearing footsteps, Polly risked a glance at the entryway. Caroline and the twins raced into the great room, eyes and mouths agape.

"Is he dead yet?" blurted Brittany.

"Is anyone hurt?" asked Bethany.

"What can we do?" said Caroline.

"Stay positive. Believe in me," said Psyche. "Please, I am serious, your thoughts and energy will keep me focused." She swooped through the air and opened a portal, blocking Nur-gahl's exit. It crackled with intensity. He rose to his feet and glared at her with malevolence.

"Listen to me, girls," Nur-gahl began.

"NO! Close your minds and ignore his words. Think of something you love instead." Psyche's voice sounded so quiet to Polly, who struggled to look away from Nick's face.

"Polly, I love you. I want you. I need you now. I need you to help me," Nur-gahl said, perfectly replicating Nick's voice. Polly was compelled. She felt an overwhelming urge to knock Psyche and Alya down and go to him.

"Polly, don't!" Bethany ran toward Polly.

"NO!" Brittany shouted, following her sister.

Nur-gahl, seeing what was about to happen, telekinetically threw the twins up and over the table and back through the room, smashing them through the huge bay window. The sound of shattering glass mingled with their screams as they cleared the deck and splashed into the cold lake outside.

Polly stepped back, and an invisible wall materialized behind her body. The force of it pressed her forward again. She tried to grip the ground with her feet, which slid helplessly along the floor. She tried to steady herself and tumbled onto the hardwood, landing on her hands and knees. She sucked in a cry of pain.

"You will all suffer more than you can possibly imagine." Nur-gahl glared at the remaining girls.

"Alya, shoot now!" Psyche yelled.

"I can't—I can't move!" Alya shouted back.

"You have to fire. He's making me want to tackle you!" Polly shouted, fighting the urge but still putting one foot slowly in front of the other.

Psyche's face contorted. She let out a guttural "URRRRRUUGGHH" as she waged an unseen battle with Nur-gahl's mind. Just then, Polly felt an invisible fist release its hold on her body and mind.

Alya fired the shotgun. The spray only partially hit her target. She quickly reached into her pocket for the salt shells. Nur-gahl grunted and shook his head, stretching his arms in spite of his wounds. Alya opened the shotgun to reload and a shard of window glass flew across the room and struck the middle of her chest. She sputtered and fell backwards.

Caroline dove toward Alya, wailing and shrieking. Nur-gahl swept an arm in her direction and Caroline slid back into the waiting portal.

"Nooooooooo!" Polly screamed as Caroline disintegrated into a silvery mist. She watched then as Psyche and Nur-gahl both instinctively opened their mouths to receive the mist, energy flowing into them. Their eyes flared with fresh power and the floor beneath them trembled.

"Polly! Grab the gun and load it! FIRE THAT WEAPON!" Psyche hollered.

Polly picked up the gun, slipping in Alya's blood as she refilled both barrels and snapped it shut. She raised the gun and fired. The salt spray missed Nur-gahl, and the recoil knocked Polly to the ground. She righted herself and fired again, and this time Psyche, using her powers, forced the salt to strike Nur-gahl. He cried out. Polly scrambled to her feet again and dug around for the remaining salt shells in Alya's jacket, shaking from shock.

Nick's body melted in a bloody mess of bone and muscle. The revolting organic pile shifted and changed, becoming, again, a massive grizzly bear. The telltale hump bristled with coarse brown spikes of slimy fur.

Psyche dissolved as well. Polly jerked her head away. She risked a peek out of the corner of her eye and saw, where a girl had been only a moment ago, a shining majestic unicorn, shaking its silky mane of satin hair and crowned with a glorious pearl horn. The animal glowed exactly as Polly had seen in the orchard, and before that in her imagination.

The bear reared up and opened its mouth. A noise like the grinding of gigantic metal gears rumbled from inside its chest, escalating to a primal roar that rattled Polly's teeth. He fell to his feet again, shaking the entire room, and reached out with one swipe to knock the mangled dining table out the bay window. Then he charged at the unicorn—at Psyche. She gracefully sidestepped the bear's attack, but in doing so bounced Polly into the wall.

Though reeling from the pain, Polly was able to think clearly. *I believe in you, Psyche. You can finish what you started so far away, in another time and place. I trust and love you.*

The unicorn stared at Polly. Her facial features did not change, but the animal's glow intensified. She reared up and charged the bear as it was in mid-swipe, aiming for Alya's unconscious body.

The strong pearl horn impaled the bear's shoulder. Her charge knocked him off balance and pushed him back. The bear grunted, pawing at the unicorn, horn still firmly lodged inside him.

Polly hurried and grabbed Alya's feet, praying she was still alive as she dragged her around the corner and away from the battle. She checked Alya's pulse as she had seen the twins do. A heartbeat—she felt a rush of hope travel through her, setting off a second torrent of tears. Polly stilled them as best she could and remembered the salt-stuffed shells in Alya's jacket.

The unicorn and bear were still wrestling as Polly reloaded the shotgun. Fear drained from her as she lifted the weapon, positioning herself next to the two struggling animals.

She lined up a shot as the pair continued to wrestle.

Psyche, I love you. Nur-gahl, I hope you find hell.

And then, barrels to the bear's skull, she pulled the trigger.

Chapter 34

Polly had been ready for the shotgun's kick; it was the wound made by the salt that shocked her. She reeled as a red crater exploded out the side of the bear's skull. Her shot was so close that the spray was focused enough to strike between his eye and ear. The morphling's vulnerability had been laid bare.

The unicorn lurched back, pulling her horn from the bear's shoulder. She flailed her blood-spattered head. Polly watched both the injured bear and the stunned unicorn scramble to right themselves. The swirling, glowing portal to another plane hung in the air mere feet away.

Psyche seized the moment and stabbed Nur-gahl again, in the center of his chest.

Polly let the shotgun fall from her hands. Shock took over—she felt as if her feet had been nailed to the ground. *Alya! Caroline! Where are the twins?* No sooner did the question leap into Polly's mind than a sopping wet pair of girls marched into the house. Swiftly, Brittany scooped up the shotgun and fired at the horn wound in the bear's chest. Nur-gahl collapsed. Polly passed more shells to Brittany, who reloaded the gun.

"Psyche, are you ready if I fire again?" Brittany said breathlessly.

The glowing unicorn shimmered, melting into a bright light that shifted shape and faded to reveal a human girl once more. "Yes. I am ready," said

Psyche, back in her human body.

Polly shielded her eyes, waiting for the blast, but saw instead a bloody blur transform into a body.

"Stand still!" yelled Brittany, aiming at a fatally wounded version of Nick. Polly had to look away from the ruin that was his face.

"Wait!" cried Nur-gahl. "I have to live. If you kill me, she is the last—and she will die alone!"

"Ignore him," blurted Psyche.

"Gladly." Brittany fired and a spray of salt hit the wailing figure that now barely resembled Nick.

The granules hissed and popped as Nur-gahl's body absorbed the mineral.

"Polly, stop them! Save me!"

Polly felt disgust and disbelief. She fought the urge to run and instead picked up a thick piece of window frame. She stepped forward and struck Nur-gahl in the head with it.

"It was not enough! Fire the salt again!" Psyche yelled, visibly straining as she concentrated.

Brittany fired. Nur-gahl morphed again, this time becoming an unrecognizable shape, black as night. He howled through an opening fringed with thousands of tiny white teeth. The noise grew louder as his mouth widened. No eyes, no features—just a gaping maw of hunger reaching up out of a puddle of ink.

Psyche summoned every drop of energy she could and shaped it into a dense blue ball of snapping electricity. The orb brightened until it was blinding, white and pure.

Polly had to shield her eyes. She watched through her fingers as Psyche launched the sphere at the dying black blob. The impact blasted the inky shadow into smoke, which Psyche telekinetically restrained and shoved into the portal.

The mass of black ooze gave one last muffled cry before dissolving into ethereal mist. Psyche struggled to force the last wisps of mist into the fissure, but it eluded her grasp. It veered up and flowed directly into her, causing her to plummet to the ground, limp. Polly rushed to Psyche's body to check for signs of life.

"Alya!" Bethany ran to where Alya was lying in a dark puddle of her own blood. Brittany dropped the shotgun and darted to her sister's side.

"She's lost a lot of blood," said Bethany, evaluating the floor.

"It must have missed her arteries, though. How is that possible?" Brittany eyed the glass shard still stuck in Alya's chest.

"Luck," Psyche said, slowly rising to her feet. "I saw the attack in Nur-gahl's mind. I used my own energy to knock it off course. I had hoped the blade would miss her." She touched Brittany's shoulder and gestured for her to move aside.

"Careful, Psyche. She might have an arterial wound." Bethany's frown deepened as Psyche pulled the glass shard out of Alya. Then, with her free hand, Psyche ripped Alya's necklace off and ate it. She covered the wound with both hands. Blood seeped through her fingers—and then stopped.

Alya sucked in a sharp gulp of air and her eyes popped open. "What happened? Where am I?"

"We're still in the lake house. We did it. He's dead," said Polly.

"Where's Caroline?"

Polly shook her head. Brittany clamped a hand over her mouth and Bethany hugged her.

"Oh, god, Caroline. What are we going to tell her parents?" Alya broke down. She sat up and put her face in her hands. "Oh my god," she said, rocking back and forth.

"I hope it was worth it. We lost our friend so you could kill your demon." Brittany wrenched herself away from her sister and shot Psyche a scathing glare.

"That thing would've gone on a killing spree. You know that," Bethany said, trying to catch her sister's eye. Brittany ignored her and marched out onto the deck.

A chilly breeze sailed up off the lake, entering through the broken bay window. Polly shivered. "Psyche, you have to do something," she said, stepping in front of the girl. "You have to get her back. We're not going to knock on our friend's door and tell her parents she's dead."

"I may actually be able to do something." Psyche moved into the space where her portal had been. She reached up and touched the empty air. "I absorbed Nur-gahl's ability to create. I might be able to use that to rebuild her."

"You have to try." Bethany's tone was firm.

Alya looked on, her face still smeared with blood.

"Stand back," Psyche said. "Get out of the room, all of you."

Polly, Alya, and Bethany quickly retreated through the front door, to where Brittany was watching from the deck.

Through the missing window, the girls watched as Psyche drew blood, bone, wood, glass, fabric, plaster, and bits of half the room into a whirling vortex. The blend of matter continued to spin, condensing and coalescing until it formed the shape of a girl.

Dust hovered artfully around the shape, slipping into edges and around curves, adding definition to eyelids, ears, a nose. Clothing settled over the shape in a layer slowly woven out of busy particles. A subtle aura of electricity shimmered as Psyche lifted one hand at where the portal had been and with the other palmed the shape's forehead, muttering something unintelligible as light seeped out from under Psyche's hand.

Psyche stepped back from her creation and looked to the other girls.

Caroline's eyes opened.

Polly released her breath.

"Dude!" Brittany shouted, clamping both hands over her mouth.

"Woah!" Bethany said, doing similarly.

"Caroline, are you okay?" Alya said breathlessly.

"I think so. Where was I? Did I go through that portal and come back?"

"In a manner of speaking." Psyche extended a hand to Caroline, who accepted. Psyche smiled and guided her to the front door.

Chapter 35

Polly's mom was asleep on the couch exactly where Polly had pictured her. Colorful bars hummed from the television. The girls flopped one after another onto cushions and chairs while Polly gently placed her precious backpack on the coffee table.

Psyche stood perfectly still next to the couch.

"Can you heal her without the silver now?" Polly's mind flashed to the scene of Alya's healing and Caroline's miraculous resurrection. She briefly pictured returning to Sun Valley Jeweler's, replacing the silver, and somehow concealing the break-in.

"I am afraid not. Rebuilding your friend depleted me almost completely despite the charge I received from Nur-gahl's essence. But I believe we do have an adequate amount of silver for this process. Take heart. She will be well soon." Psyche smiled warmly.

"Do you have to wake her up?" Polly's voice shook as she rubbed bloodshot eyes.

"No, she is in a deep sleep. Her calm works in our favor." Psyche gently placed an open palm on Polly's mom's forehead, and then touched her patient's chest. Psyche's brow furrowed as though processing complicated information.

Polly's eyes filled to the brim with tears. *It's finally happening,* she thought.

Mom's really going to get better.

Psyche reached for the table and opened the backpack. She casually shoveled silver finger rings, charms, and chains into her mouth like handfuls of popcorn.

Brittany and Bethany sat up on their floor cushions. Alya and Caroline leaned forward in their chairs. Psyche closed her eyes and mouth in a moment of meditation. Then: white light burst in thick shafts from her eyelids and nostrils. She crouched next to Polly's mom and carefully pried open her sleeping mouth. Psyche leaned in, almost kissing her, and focused all her light into a single beam, directing it into Polly's mom.

Liquid light poured from the morphling girl until the energy was depleted. Psyche moved her hands around Polly's mom's body, touching her forehead, smoothing her hair, gripping her shoulders, caressing her stomach, and finally whisking something invisible off her mom's legs.

"Did it work?" Polly gripped the couch arm above her mom's head.

"I wonder what our parents would say about this particular branch of medicine," said Bethany to her sister.

"They'd say it's time for us to go home." Alya reached out to Caroline, who still seemed confused and lightly stunned. "Of course, I'll need to change first." Alya lifted the bottom of her slashed and bloody shirt.

"Upstairs in my room. Anything that fits is yours." Polly grinned ecstatically.

Psyche gazed patiently at Polly's happy, yet frazzled, expression. "I will drive you all home. Polly and I must also return that van."

"Of course!" Polly said. "That would have sucked, getting caught after everything that's happened." She followed as her friends filed back out the front door.

"You still might get caught," cautioned Caroline.

"But it won't be because of us." Alya reappeared in the living room, smiling in one of Polly's geometric button-up shirts. Tingles of relief prickled down Polly's back.

Another week of school passed with Psyche coming and going at Polly's side.

Psyche had agreed to stay until the next weekend, just in case Polly or one of her friends had a visit from local law enforcement. Neither were sure what Psyche could accomplish—memory alteration, hypnosis, or simply taking the fall and slipping out of this dimension through a jail cell wall. Endless possibilities bounced between them during their walks up Sagebrush Ridge to the little orchard house where Polly's mom was supervising a small crew of carpenters fixing their west wall.

"Let's have our dinner in the backyard tonight. It's not super warm, but the patio furniture should be dry. And the kitchen smells like that caulk they've been using on the windows and the sliding glass door," Polly said to Psyche as she unpacked cardboard boxes of fried chicken from plastic grocery bags and restacked them on the kitchen counter.

"Yes, I think I would like to eat outside. This will be my last meal with you. It should be special." Psyche gently guided her curtain of blonde hair back over her shoulder.

"Already? It's Friday night. You were supposed to stay for the weekend," whined Polly.

"Using a grating tone of voice will not change my plans. I have kept all my promises to you, Polly Michaels. It is time for me to return to the Astral Temple."

"To do what? Sit there alone for the rest of time? I still don't get it, Psyche. Why not stay here with me? You need some people. I need more than one family member." Polly weighed the air with empty palms, cocking one eyebrow at Psyche. "Sounds like a good fit to me."

"I will say again that I do not 'need' people. I do not belong here. I do not belong in a world where people live and die in bodies of meat."

"Ugh, Psyche, you make us sound like cattle. But don't elaborate. I don't need more detail."

Polly arranged plates, cutlery, and boxes of fast food in a tower and carried them in her arms. "Can you get the door?" she asked, adding with a whisper, "Let's go enjoy your last taste of mortal food."

Once outside, relentless banging resumed and assaulted their ears directly. Polly's mom grabbed a greasy drumstick from the top takeout box as Polly and Psyche passed through the chaos of hammering and drills. The girls settled into their makeshift picnic nearby and Polly watched Psyche's slow, bite-by-bite progress.

"Psyche, have you really found nothing in our world—or any other you've seen—that makes you want to be alive? Really living and experiencing and enjoying . . . everything? Anything at all in the whole universe?"

Psyche chewed away on a piece of buttermilk biscuit before taking a sip of cola. She shot a startled glare at the carbonated liquid.

"I do enjoy experiencing new worlds and forms." She burped and covered her mouth. Her cheeks went pink with embarrassment. "But I think you still do not comprehend what I am and how long I have existed. Nothing that has happened to me in the last couple of weeks has changed the nature of . . . me."

"Okay. Fine. But would you at least consider coming back one day?"

"All right, I will come back. At some point."

Polly leaned back in the cold mesh of her patio chair and smiled. Securing Psyche's potential return constituted a victory. A few moments later, a dark cloud passed over Polly's head.

"I think I get where you're coming from," she said, leaning forward. "If you stay here and get more attached, you'll have to lose me when I grow old and die. You can't spend your time looking after me either. And neither can my mom. Not forever. Even though she's all right now, I'm still going to lose her one day. I need to be able to handle loss. On my own."

"All things must cope with loss. Few do it well."

"I won't do it well." Polly dropped a partially eaten chicken breast to her plate and wiped her fingers with a paper napkin. "I still miss my dad. It makes me angry that I can't remember him as well as I used to. I can't hear his voice in my head. I can't picture his face clearly without a photograph. People used to tell me that I'd feel better after time, even if I had to wait years. But in reality, it's like he's slipping away from me forever."

Polly's gut expanded as though her biscuits were giving her indigestion. Psyche took a careful sip of her drink and met Polly's sour gaze.

Can you tell me what happens to my species when we die? Is Heaven real? Is there another dimension where departed souls go? Is there a place like the Astral Temple for dead humans? Polly couldn't bring herself to say the words out loud, despite being sure the carpenters' tools gave her privacy from her mom's ears.

"Polly, if I knew, I would tell you, I promise. But I do not have answers of that nature for you. Even the archives my people built over eons do not encompass everything that ever has been or ever will be. I do know that the entirety of existence is so complex that no one consciousness could ever understand it all. There is no all-encompassing explanation. In my personal opinion, of course."

Polly's stomach rumbled. Around the corner, one of the circular saws screeched as it bit hard on a nail. Both girls cringed.

"I almost forgot—I have something I want to give you. A small gift to remember me by." Polly reached into her jeans pocket and pulled out her mother's mood stone earrings. She handed the intact one to Psyche. "Mom let me have these when we were tidying up her dresser the other day. I gave them to her for Christmas when I was little and one of them broke soon afterwards. They're cheaply made, but they're fun. Watch this." Polly closed her fist around her charm and blew warm air onto the stone. She opened her hand and the stone was glowing aqua-blue.

"How delightful!" Psyche smiled in amusement. "And this is for me to keep?"

"I know you probably can't take it with you when you go, but I figured it's the thought that counts." Polly's brow furrowed as she looked at Psyche. Polly tried to picture her unicorn drawings again to bury her worry that this gift was lame.

"I love it! Truly. And I have a gift for you in return." Psyche held out her hand to Polly, gesturing for the other earring. Confused, Polly complied anyway.

Psyche cupped both earrings in her hands and brought them to her mouth. She exhaled on the charms and a blue glow illuminated Psyche's hands. Polly's eyes widened. Her gaze darted to her mom and the workers, but everyone was busy examining the door frame.

Psyche opened her hands. The old pewter frames were gone. The mood stones gleamed at the heart of two geometric copper settings like sunbursts of arrows. Both stones were a bright fuchsia.

"Whoa! That's fantastic." Polly accepted her new-old pendant back.

"Now they are authentically symbols from both our worlds." Psyche smiled and placed her pendant on the table next to her plate of food. She resumed eating with a thoughtful calm demeanor.

"Psyche?"

"Yes?"

"Wanna stay up and watch *The Tonight Show* with me?"

"All right."

"Can you wait until I fall asleep to leave? I can't watch you go."

"Of course, Polly."

A chilly wind blew through them. Polly collected their plates. Psyche followed her inside while Polly's mom smiled lovingly from afar.

Epilogue

The front door opened. Polly looked away from the game show on television. She turned off the TV and stood up.

"How did it go?" She beamed at her mom, already knowing what she'd say.

"I still can't believe it."

"So . . . all better?"

"Dr. Johnson has no idea what happened. He called it a case of spontaneous remission." She set her purse down on the coffee table and kissed the top of Polly's head.

"Is that the end of it?" Polly wrapped her mom in a firm hug.

"He almost wanted to give me another round of chemo for good measure."

"What did you say to that?"

"I told him I'd take my chances without it."

Polly and her mom turned toward the sound of frantic footsteps skittering along the upstairs hall.

"Remind me why we need this dog?" Polly asked as the footsteps thumped down the stairwell behind her.

"Security, of course. We've been over this." Her mom vigorously rubbed their new Labrador puppy's head. "They coyotes were one thing, but a grizzly bear is another."

"It was a freak migration from the mountains. The parks officer told me so. And it's dead. The cops ruled the incident at the vet as an act of vandalism." Polly squared her shoulders.

"Everyone knows that's only because they never found the bear. But I'm glad you feel safe. I, on the other hand, need a little something extra. I'm the mother—it's my job to protect you." Her mom leaned in to the puppy's face and it licked her happily.

"He doesn't look like much security to me."

"Not yet, but he will. Have faith."

"Okay then, let's name him." Polly relented and scratched the cheerful dog's ear.

"How about Rover?" Her mom smiled.

"Seriously? Try something original."

"Luath."

"What?"

"For his name. Luath . . . from *The Incredible Journey*."

"Kind of a funny name, isn't it?" Polly wrinkled her nose.

She wanted to name the dog after the Astral Temple in Psyche's memory. She had told her mom that Psyche's family abruptly moved back to Sweden and tried to let the topic of her lost friend fade into history.

"How about Astro. Like an astronaut, adventuring in space," Polly said, cringing at the cheesy image of a dog in a space suit.

"Astro? All right, I think that's doable." Her mom scratched the puppy's belly. "Hello there, Astro. What do you think of your new name?" The puppy let out a small bark.

"There, see, he likes it." Polly turned the television back on. Her mom picked up the remote and turned it off again.

"Nope, we're going to Poplar Grove Park. Astro needs a run."

"He's got the whole orchard to run through! And the hills." Polly stared longingly at the television.

"I'm not having him shot at in the orchard or snapped at by coyotes in the hills."

"Is he our security or not?"

"He's a puppy, and we need to keep him safe until he's big and properly trained."

"Fair enough. Let's go." Polly shouldered her purse and followed her mom to the car. Astro jumped up onto the plaid blanket placed across the back seat as if it had always been his territory.

Poplar Grove Park was busy that Saturday, and Polly's mom had her hands full keeping Astro from eating off picnic tables and chewing on stray toys. They reached the long sandy beach beyond the tree line and Polly let them both run ahead. Her mom was so full of life these days that it overwhelmed her to think about how close she'd come to losing her.

Polly sat on a wood bench facing the lone craggy mountain on the other side of Crescent Lake. She was contemplating the stubbornness of the small cap of snow that had spent all summer clinging to its peak when someone sat down next to her.

"Penny for your thoughts?" Nick Hauser clasped his hands in his lap.

"Uh, hi, Nick." Polly shifted in her seat.

"I hear your mom is better now. That's great news."

"Yeah, we were pretty worried there. Looks like it's all sorted out now." She stole a quick glance at Nick's profile. He kept his eyes on the mountain ahead as if scrutinizing it.

"I heard you got a dog, too. I figured you'd bring him here on a Saturday. I've been waiting almost an hour already."

"Waiting for what?" Polly's heart thumped hard.

"You." Nick leveled a contemplative gaze at Polly. He didn't look away. She felt her face growing hotter. "I was thinking . . . you wanna go out to the Rack Shack tonight?"

"Oh. Um . . . yeah. I mean yes, of course."

"Good. I'll pick you up at seven." Nick stood and grinned at her. Static filled her ears. For a blink she thought it was the sound of angst. Then a blue flash drew her focus to the hillside. Electricity bloomed in a small dome at the edge of Lakeside Hills orchard.

"What on Earth is that?" Nick squinted at the hill. The electricity died down.

"The newspaper called it a pyrocumulus cloud." Polly stood up, beaming, and flung her arms around Nick's neck. "But to me, it's a miracle."

About the Author

Christine Hart is a copywriter, metalsmith, and mother who writes speculative fiction for young readers. Her backlist includes the NA trilogy, The Variant Conspiracy. Her debut YA, Watching July, won a gold medal from the Moonbeam Children's Book Awards. She holds a BA in English and Professional Writing, as well as current membership with the Federation of BC Writers and SF Canada. When not writing, she creates wearable art from recycled metals under the guise of an Etsy alter-ego **Sleepless Storyteller**. She shares her eclectic home with her husband and two children.

Watching July

Sixteen-year-old July MacKenzie adjusts from the loss of her mother and their urban lifestyle in Vancouver to a rural corner of the BC Interior.

As July meets her first love and rebuilds her life, she is forced to confront the truth about her mother's death … and the danger she still faces.